T0208113

CRUSANO

UNREWARDED FAITHFULNESS EQUALS SELF-DECEPTION

JAY LIM

For book orders, email orders@traffordpublishing.com.sg

Most Trafford Singapore titles are also available at major online book retailers.

This is a work of fiction. All of the characters, names, incidents, organizations, and dialogue in this novel are either the products of the author's imagination or are used fictitiously.

Printed in Singapore.

ISBN: 978-1-4669-2666-0 (sc)
ISBN: 978-1-4669-2667-7 (hc)
ISBN: 978-1-4669-2668-4 (e)

Trafford rev. 05/07/2012

Singapore
toll-free: 800 101 2656 (Singapore)
Fax: 800 101 2656 (Singapore)

"Gaining power and status is a personality amplifier;
it will show us the true character of a person; the kind uses
it for generosity, and the unkind uses it for corruption."

About the Author

Jay Lim now studies at the National University of Singapore. Writing fiction and philosophies have always been his interest eversince a child. He is enthusiatic about relating his fictional stories to questioning and exploring the true human nature in this real world and in today's modern society.

PREFACE

I SINCERELY THANK you for reading this book. Although it may be a short fictional novella, I hope that it will entertain you. But most importantly, this book shares with you the true nature of people—everyone is driven by self-interest, even the kindest of actions. For example, some people do the good just because they want reciprocation or perhaps, they want to make themselves feel better. Unfortunately, there are very few true Samaritans right now since the altruism does not benefit our personal survival.

But at the end of day, just be true to yourself and help others in need whenever you can. Although faithful altruism may not guarantee rewards, ultimately I believe there is a great being out there controlling this universe. And whenever we do the good, he will smile at us. And we will miraculously feel happy ourselves. Such is the true meaning of living the human life.

Now, I shall take on my alter-ego as Koby Sleuth in this adventure . . .

PROLOGUE

A DARK SHADOWY figure sped out of the darkness without a sound until it was almost behind its preys. When the couple sensed its sinister presence, they nervously spun their heads around to catch a glimpse of their stalker, but to no avail. They firmly held their hands together and started increasing their pace. Words of prayer mumbled from their mouths with the hope that Crusano will save them from this imminent danger. The night was no longer a place for the defenseless. But it was neither street muggers nor thugs that they feared.

It was the demon they feared.

The couple breathed a sigh of relief as they stepped out of the dark and gloomy alleyway. The amber glow from the streetlamps lit their world far away from darkness. They looked at each other in the eyes comfortably and smiled. Then, their hands parted as they bade farewell and started making their way home.

Just as they moved off into different directions, the man heard a terrible scream which filled the night air. It was the voice of his girlfriend. He immediately turned and ran back to look for her. He knew she was in danger.

"Gwen! Gwendoline!" He called out to her in fear and darted around the empty streets. There was no one there to help him.

He sprinted back into the deserted alley where they had passed as he sensed the assailant's presence within it. True enough, he saw Gwendoline being forcefully dragged in deeper into the darkness by a brutish arm. She was gasping for air with her eyes wide opened and her head was bleeding profusely.

When she saw her terrified boyfriend standing at the end of the alley, she used her remaining breath to shout at him to ask him to run for his life. Within a matter of seconds, the pitch black darkness swallowed her and then, she was gone.

Something emerged out of the darkness. It was a humanoid figure dressed in a black robe. The cloak made its body seemed tall while the hood covered the upper half of its pale face. Its mouth was visible, which clearly expressed a sly grin coated with crimson red liquid trickling down to its chin.

Blood. Gwendoline's blood.

Upon raising its head, the intimidating sight of its malevolent eyes came into view. There was neither an iris nor pupil in each eye. It was just the plain white sclera with red shot cracks seeping out from the sides.

It was angry. It was hungry.

Gently using its sleeves to wipe off the blood stains and small chunks of flesh crowded around its lips, it released a deafening and unearthly shriek. Its mouth opened about twenty centimeters wide, exposing its full set of razor sharp teeth. Before the young man could even react, it bolted towards him with an unnaturally fast speed and delivered a bite to his head as it fed on its prey . . .

I jolted out of my bed in cold sweat. My fingers swept across my forehead to remove a layer of it. It felt much wetter compared to the several previous nights when I had experienced the same traumatic nightmare over and over again.

The alarm system in my analog watch has never failed to pull me out from these horrible experiences. It promptly beeps at fifteen minutes past seven every morning without fail as I had set it to be since I must wake up to get to college on time. More than being my savior from nightmares, I also loved this watch for its unique design—silver chrome plated layers of mesh which firmly wrapped around my wrist. The round clock had a gold tint around it. And beneath the clock arms, there was a cyan sword engraved on the surface. It was the religious symbol of Crusano, the god of love and peace.

I jumped off the bed and slipped into my crimson T-shirt along with a pair of jeans. I walked out of the room and saw Auntie Joan placing a plate of breakfast on the wooden table. She had brown shoulder length hair, which was firmly combed to the sides. The white apron which she wore was stained with an artistic collage of tomato, barbecue and chili sauce. She smiled at me and told me to enjoy the meal before she walked back into the kitchen for some cleaning up.

I picked up a fork from the table mat and used it to swoop a slice of omelet into my mouth. It tasted the same everyday—the same type of love that a mother has for a child, the love which I am not supposed to enjoy after the death of my parents in a tragic accident when I was only five. While all other relatives shunned the responsibility to raise this orphan child, my father's younger sister proved to be different.

Despite having three children left behind by her late husband, Auntie Joan did not hesitate to raise a fourth. Although her salary as a clerk in a nearby hotel was peanuts, she was always willing to sacrifice her own needs to equally provide the best for her foster child and biological children. I believe that Auntie Joan might be one of the angels sent by Crusano, if he does really exist.

Upon finishing the last bit of the omelet, I made it out to the front door of the apartment after calling out a bid of farewell to Auntie Joan. I bent down to reach for the shoe rack outside for my pair of sneakers. It was in a mess with shoes, sandals, slippers and . . . Sprawns?

These tiny round beetle-like pests were spitting out slimy black residues to form their personal nest among the shoes.

Wait. There were one, two, three, four . . . six Sprawns together! This was a shocking sight. Sprawns were well-known territorial creatures, which were only expected to be sighted alone as it instinctively eats any other insect within a radius of two metres, including another one of its own kind.

Apart from the bizarre sight of nature that astounded me, I became rather worried about the supernatural aspect of this phenomenal. The elder folks believed that Sprawns are the bringer of misfortune. Finding one or two together should be considered normal but finding three or more together symbolizes the advent of a great calamity.

"Wow! Six at once! This is going online and fame will be all mine!" exclaimed my younger cousin Winston as he whipped out his phone and started filming those six little pests with glee.

Winston was the youngest son of Auntie Joan. He was eight years old with a mop of dark brown unkempt hair and chubby fair cheeks. To me, he resembled a little pig from the cartoons on Saturday mornings. His hyper activeness was a double-edged sword, it could brighten up your day one moment and it might also turn out to be extremely irritating and infuriating. But nevertheless, I always loved him as a younger brother.

"Stop it! This is not funny!" I told him off as I raised my hand to block his phone's camera. "Don't you remember what our late grandpa shared with us when visited him for the last time five years ago?"

I knew I was too foolish to ask; firstly, Winston might not even be able remember what grandpa said since he was only three years old back then. Secondly, he might be too immature to even understand that there are some things which we must never ever play or joke around with, especially when it concerns the supernatural, spiritual or simply whatever laws which are beyond our human control.

Even though I was not the hardcore superstitious sort of person, I kept my fingers crossed all the way to college during my bus trip nonetheless. It was better to be safe than sorry. The coincidental combination of the horrible nightmares and the bad omen from the Sprawns gave me goose bumps all over my body. I tried to stop thinking about it, because if I was to allow this "bad luck" notion to be stuck in my head, it may actually turn out to be a self-fulfilled prophecy. Hence, I read my notes on physics to get my thoughts focused on something less disturbing until I arrived at college.

The national college of Eropagnis was probably the best in Eropagnis city. It was a large campus with a grand quadrangle built within the heart of the school compound. There were about a thousand students in total, who were divided into different classes based on their subject combinations. During the start of the academic year, I chose to be in the engineering class.

Most of the students aimed for popular classes such as medicine and law which would offer them the most prestigious jobs in the future, namely doctors and lawyers respectively. Although I did score well enough during my entrance exam to be able enter these top-notch classes, I eventually went for engineering class as there was a special someone whom I wanted to see every day in class. Also, being an engineer wasn't too bad due the uprising of many technological industries.

She sat diagonally in front of me during class. I was always looking at her—ogling at her actually—from behind. Her jet black hair with a long ponytail along with her attractive and delicate features made her the key attention to most boys in the college, and I was one of them.

More than just the physical attraction, I was most attracted to her kind, independent and selfless nature.

During a camping trip back in the first year of middle school, I was on the verge of dying twice after several bullies humiliated me by rendering me stark naked in front of everyone. The experience was sick. First, I tried to take my own life by attempting to swallow some poisonous berries found near our camp site. Just then, one of the girls from the other class slapped the berries off my hands and started to preach on how foolish it would be for me to end my life. She looked very angry and upset, but at the same time, I knew she felt sorry for me.

Later that night, I noticed students passing subtle remarks to each other and they were giggling. It soon became clear that I was the main topic of their little joke. They said insulting and disgusting remarks such as how my pubic area looked like and whether I would be able to attract a female bear. Without thinking rationally, I ran straight into the forest with embarrassment and pain in my heart. I just want to get away from this bunch of uncivilised scumbags.

After several minutes of blind scurrying through the forest, I soon came to realize that I had indeed got away from those rascals, but unfortunately, I got away too far from the camp site. As I turned back to retrace my steps, all I saw was nothing except trees and bushes, which were barely visible under the pale moonlight. I trekked my way around aimlessly for several minutes, and then there was a figure crashing through the trees right in front me.

"Idiot! What were you thinking? Do you know how dangerous it is to come out here alone in the night?" the angry voice was familiar. It was the same girl who had spoiled my suicidal attempt earlier that day. I remained silent.

"And when you get lost in the forest, you will be an easy prey for some nocturnal predators!" She held her breath for a moment, and then she looked around and continued. "Well, I guess we are both lost and easy preys for nocturnal predators."

Such a ditzy girl! I thought. I initially wanted to tell her off for being a busybody. But then, I had to see the other side of the story; she might have seen me running away into the forest and hence, she pursued me immediately without taking a compass as any moment of delay meant that she would not be able to catch up. So I asked myself whether I should be grateful for her courageous yet foolish act. I came to understand that we were both equally foolish.

For the next few minutes, or hours, we navigated our way through the forested labyrinth but to no avail. Soon, we managed to find a small little cave in the undergrowth which provided us ample shelter for the night.

The night air was freezing and without the tools to start a fire, the both of us had to endure the bitter cold that cruelly seeped through our thin skin. The clothing which we wore in the day barely kept us warm after nightfall. The problem with such forests during this season would be the extreme temperature during the day, and its complete opposite during the night.

I was excruciatingly fatigue, but my hunger and the coldness deliberately stopped me from getting any rest. My hands were shivering as I clasped them together and started rubbing. Every bit of warmth was essential to keep me away from frostbites. Suddenly, there was a slight warmer feeling spreading across my shoulders. I looked over to my left shoulder and there was a dark blue jacket resting comfortably on it.

It belonged to that girl.

"Don't you feel cold?" I asked her for the sake of asking. Of course she was feeling cold!

Without looking in my direction, she simply shook her head as she positioned herself to lie down on the muddy ground. I covered her shoulders with the jacket and leaned down about two metres away from her. Aunt Joan constantly reminded me that physical boundaries are important between genders of an opposite sex, unless there is an intimate relationship of sort.

While struggling to keep my cupped hands warm by blowing into it, I felt a pair of gentle arms wrapping around my torso. I nearly jumped up like a scalded cat when I realized that she was hugging me from behind.

"Relax. Turn back and do the same. This will keep us both warm and alive till tomorrow morning." She instructed me. Her voice sounded reluctant.

I did as what I was told and our faces came close together. She looked even more beautiful close-up with the flawless skin and remarkable features. Her dark brown eyes looked down and avoided mine. She ought to be feeling just as uncomfortable as I was. Therefore, I decided to start a conversation.

I asked for her name. Yes, that was what most boys would ask whenever they meet a pretty girl they do not know.

"Gwendoline. Gwendoline Nightingale," She said. Coincidentally, the male nightingales were singing beautifully on the tree canopies above us. "You are?"

"Koby. Koby Sleuth." I introduced myself.

"Sleuth? You mean like a detective? Wow!" She said with amusement. Then, she kept quiet for a moment and closed her eyes, before clutching her hands together and started murmuring.

Despite our close distance, I could barely hear what she was saying or doing. I had to ask her.

"I was praying to Crusano, the god of love and peace," She exuberantly replied, as though she had found new strength from her prayer. "I prayed to Crusano. I prayed that he will lead us back to our camp."

Crusano. I have heard of that name. In fact, everyone in the world knew who he was. In the influential religion known as Crusanity, the Followers depicted Crusano as a divine being that had once came to our realm during the ancient times to save mankind from a devastating calamity. In his interaction with mankind, he took the form of a handsome man dressed in shiny white and blue armor and he wielded a cyan sword. The sword, according to what I have read, was not used for killing but rather, it was meant to protect those who worshipped him.

Gwendoline was undeniably one of the fervent believers. As for the non-religious me, well, I only read up on these facts for personal knowledge, nothing more than that.

That morning, Gwendoline and I "miraculously" found our way back to the campsite. After we received a good scolding from the teachers-in-charge, Gwendoline thanked and praised Crusano for bringing us back safe and sound. I was rather annoyed by it actually. I believed that it was the sunlight and the ample amount of rest that led us back to our camp and not some kind of spiritual force. If Crusano was indeed some kind of powerful god, he should have teleported us back last night to save us from those nefarious mosquitoes and bitter frost!

I was shaken out of my flashback when the college bell rang. School was finally over for the day. As I packed up to leave the classroom, Gwendoline walked up beside me and reminded me to join the congregation tomorrow as one of our church friends Pierre, would be sharing his testimony about Crusano.

"Oh, is it about how Crusano divinely made a turning point in his life?" I asked Gwendoline with hints of sarcasm.

After the incident back in middle school, Gwendoline had invited me to join the Love of Crusano church. I gladly took up the offer and became a Follower myself, not because I believe in Crusano but rather, I wanted to see Gwendoline more frequently. Yes, I was very childish and madly in love with her. Perhaps, this was part of growing up as a teenager.

"Come on Koby, it is not easy for Pierre to speak in front of so many people at the congregation," Gwendoline exclaimed; she must have sensed my sarcasm. "We must give him our support and encouragement."

I laughed and nodded my head. Just then, a serious issue came into my mind and decided to bring it up to Gwendoline.

"Gwen, I heard some of our church members died recently from some accidents. Pastor Darmor said that they are the backsliders who chose to deny Crusano's protection. Do you think . . ."

"Don't worry! Crusano will protect us as long as we seek his salvation." She confidently interrupted me. "Even the Shadow will not dare to lay a hair on us."

I kept my mouth shut. The accidents were horrible. The latest news reported one of the victims got fatally stung by a swarm of hornets. Indeed, he was misfortunate.

He may have rattled the hornets' nest. I thought, although many people at church suspected him to be a victim of Avor's servant, a demonic entity known as Shadow.

According to Crusanity religious doctrines, it was mentioned that the god Crusano had archenemy known as Avor. It was the cursed master of hatred and destruction. During the period of the Great Ancient War when mankind was placed on the verge of extinction, Avor was supposedly destroyed by Crusano. But unfortunately, the doctrines warned us that Avor's most dreaded servant, the Shadow, still lurked among us to carry out its master's goal by preying on Crusano's people, the Followers.

But after the dawn of science, only the Followers believed in such historical fact whereas in the eyes of the others who shunned religion, it was merely a myth. As for myself, I was just curious as to whether such spiritual stuffs still dwelled covertly among us since there was no scientific proof that they exist.

Gwendoline and I made our way out of the classroom just as our classmate Jack Mania hopped up in front of us. He was a muscular young man, slightly taller than I was but he was packed three times more muscles. His scruffy moustache was an eyesore for the teachers in college; being in one of the best schools in Eropagnis city, the grooming standards had to be equally stellar. Yet, he did nothing about it. But since he was the one of the top students in college, the teachers decided to pardon him.

Despite being a very intelligent young man, he was very eccentric—you do not need to know him well to realize this. Jack often advertised his ghost busting and demon trapping services during class by handing out brochures and offering discounts for packages. And it served out well to be a free entertainment service for the class as we would laugh at him for such idiotic act. I loved it whenever I asked him how many customers did he have and he would reply me, "Ten. Ten deducted by ten customers in total!"

He was obviously kidding me.

Just as I was about to ask him the same jesting question, Gwendoline tapped me in the head with a pen.

"Jack needs psychological help okay? It's not funny whenever you play along with him, just to make fun of him." Gwendoline harshly whispered to me. Then she turned to Jack.

"It's okay Jack. We don't really need your professional services. But you can always teach us physics when you are available." Gwendoline smiled at Jack. Hence, Jack nodded with a smile. Rearranging his brochures, he moved off to seek other potential customers who were within his sight. Henceforth, most people made themselves invisible to him.

I apologised to Gwendoline. She never liked it whenever I teased others. She was indeed a very serious person. But to me, she was very charming with such an attitude.

"Apology accepted if tonight's dinner is on you." She demanded with a cheeky grin on her face.

I eagerly complied. Another opportunity to go out with her!

The food at Chopper's Cafe was pretty appetizing, especially bolognaise with minced meat and mozzarella cheese. It was Gwendoline's favourite, not mine. But still, I gobbled it down for the day's hunger. No, in fact, I was trying to eat like a young gentleman with proper table manners as she was sitting right in front of me and facing me. I did not want to make myself look like some sort of untidy caveman.

"Hey, there is a speck of tomato sauce on your chin." Gwendoline pointed out. As I took a piece of cloth from the table and started wiping that area, she gave a hoot and grabbed the cloth to assist me in wiping it off. Perhaps being an untidy caveman was not too bad.

My smile was broken when I caught a glimpse of a figure standing outside the cafe. It was a tall and dark silhouette. Although I was unable to make out any facial features, I swore it was staring right at me through the cafe's window. Then, it raised its hand and started waving at me! I jumped out of my seat.

"Yikes! Kob, are you okay?" Gwendoline was startled.

"Gwen! Look! Who or what in the world is that?" I exclaimed. But when I looked up again, it was gone. It vanished into thin air. I ran out of the front door towards the alley and spun my head around in all directions. There was nothing at all. The alley was empty. Even if the mysterious figure was to sprint straight down the alleyway into the main streets, I ought to be able to see him since the alleyway was too long, narrow and straight. I was wondering how it was possible for anyone to disappear out of sight within three seconds.

As I walked back to our table, Gwendoline shot me with a puzzled look. I told her that it might have been my imagination. She told me that she had heard some church members who had the same experience recently. She continued to explain how demonic forces would try to frighten us for being a Follower but also assured me that Crusano would always protect us from any harm as long as we are faithful to him.

"Then what about those who kicked the bucket recently?" I blurted out while trying to recover from my shock.

"But those are the backsliders right? They chose to neglect Crusano's protection." She explained. "Crusano will protect us. Don't worry and go get some rest okay? And thank you for the dinner treat."

At that point, I was neither afraid of ghost stalking me nor demonic forces trying to kill me, for not having enough faith in Crusano. I was merely surprised and mystified by the enigmatic figure.

With Gwendoline waiting for me outside, I went into the gents to wash my face. The toilet was empty and quite filthy but it did not matter to me. After throwing waves of sink water to the face, I went to the urinal to take a leak. And when I got back to the sink to wash my hands, I nearly fainted upon the sight of words scribbled on the mirror.

I am watching you. It read.

They were scribbled in crimson red. The colour was a little too dark for markers and a little too bright for inks.

It was *blood*, justified by the rusting smell diffusing from it.

I screamed at the top of my voice and I felt as if I was about to vomit my heart out. Upon recalling the horrible nightmares and bad omen, my level of fear shot up sky high. I felt angry and irritated. This had to be some prankster's sick joke on me. The words were not there one moment and the next moment, it appeared! How could it be possible? What about the shadowy figure I saw earlier on? Was it behind this?

The cafe owner Miss Paige Chopper, a tall, slim and fair lady rushed into the gents.

"Your friend and I heard you screaming from outside. What happened?" And when she noticed the writing on the mirror, she exclaimed, "What is this?"

While trying to regain my breath, I asked her whether anyone came in to the gents during the past few minutes.

"No. You and your friend are the last customers here! If you did not scribble this piece of shit, some clown must have done it earlier today!" Miss Chopper grunted before taking up a wet cloth with her hand. She was wrong. It was not scribbled earlier today—it was done when I was taking leak—by someone or something.

Miss Chopper began cleaning off the stains and cursing as I left the gents feeling pale. I doubt Miss Chopper even realized it was actually blood that she was wiping. When Gwendoline asked me what happened inside, I merely told her, "Someone did not flush the toilet bowl."

Just as I was about to be convinced that it was a indeed supernatural being attempting to haunt me, the ghost busting, demonic trapping and eccentric Jack came to my mind.

He has to be the culprit! I thought. *Perhaps this was one of his gimmicks to entice me to buy his services!*

Love of Crusano

It was already past midnight when I foraged through my bedroom for the name card, the one that was badly printed in blue with Jack's contact number on it. Jack distributed tons of it to me and every classmate daily but when I needed it now, I could not even find one. After almost an hour of scavenging, I finally found that piece of crumpled junk under my bed.

I was greeted by a happy and excited voice when I dialed the number. Jack ought to be expecting a new customer. A new customer indeed if I was dumb enough to be fooled by his gimmicks. So I went straight to the point.

"You think stalking me and writing those words will scare me?" I growled furiously. Honestly saying, I was afraid. The nightmares that I experienced along with the inauspicious omen might be a tell-tale sign of an advent curse. And now this fool played a joke on me?

"What are you talking about man? Jack didn't scare you. Jack is just making a living off Jack's interest. So don't come and accuse me of some crap." His voice sounded convincing, but not convincing enough for me.

"Whatever! Look, just stop playing ghost to frighten me, Gwen or any classmates you hear me? If not, I will tell the teachers at college and they will suspend you." I threatened. "Or worst, I will call the police to charge you for harassment!"

"Darn it is not Jack! Koby, please listen. If you really are running into those "things", just let Jack know, Jack can help you. And of course, give you a good discount for it. Okay?" Jack seemed to be concern about me. I could hear it through his voice. But wait, he was supposed to be concern about my situation in the first place! It was another one of his "brilliant" marketing strategies, very similar to governmental election periods when corrupt politicians gained support by pretending to be concern for the well-being of the people.

"I think I've made my point. Enough with those jokes. I will not mind paying you tuition fees if you can coach me in physics, but what you are doing now is way too much." I felt calmer upon recalling what Gwendoline told me about the possible tragic that gave Jack his eccentric nature.

I should not be angry with him. I told myself.

Jack lost his parents two years ago when a killer tsunami crashed into their beach vacation which was meant to be a joyous occasion. He suffered a greater ordeal than I did; I barely remembered my parents since I was too young during the tragedy, whereas Jack witnessed the tidal waves taking the lives of his parents. And I had a loving Aunt Joan to take of care me, whereas Jack had to fend for himself by doing various odd jobs to financially provide for his basic needs and pay off his hefty education fees. His determination was admirable.

"Come on man! Jack is one hundred percent innocent! Never mind, if you really need help in physics, Jack can give you free tuition. But please, believe me! Jack is not playing a prank on you," Jack explained. I fell silent. "Koby? Koby? You there?"

I froze. My fingers shivered. My phone came crashing down onto the ground. The same silhouette was outside my window. Its head stuck out from below. This time, I saw its eyes—yellow iris with blood-shot red sclera—glaring at me. Impossible! I told myself. I was living on the sixteenth floor in this apartment block. Surely no one would be able to defy gravity with their head showing up outside the window!

I dared not do anything but stood rigid and hoped that "thing" would go away and above all, not harm anyone including myself. For that very moment, I placed aside my non-religious nature to mouth a quiet prayer to Crusano to ask for his protection against this demonic entity. And as if on cue, the dark figure's head sank down and out of sight. I breathed a sigh of relief.

For the rest of the night, I was afraid to be alone. Hence, I went to my cousins' room to sleep. So there were four of us cramming inside a small room; Winston, Kylee, Nicholas and myself. Initially, I was expecting the naughty little Winston to decline my request to sleep in their room. But thankfully, he actually agreed to it. No doubt, he was under the influence of his more sensible and helpful siblings.

I laid beside Winston and Nicholas on the floor mattress whereas Kylee, being the only girl, took the bed. After the terrifying sightings, I was unable to catch a wink. Even if I was able to get some shut-eye, I would be plagued by the same nightmare; the dark alley, Gwendoline's scream, the humanoid-like demon with fangs. My rest was badly disrupted as I jolted out of bed almost every instant I slipped into oblivion. I asked myself whether I might be suffering from psychological disorder. The symptoms were too great to ignore. And before having a chance to take a nap, the dawn approaches.

The day was less frightening than the night. I had the confidence that the sunlight will fend off any spiritual darkness; when light and darkness are together in the same space and time, only light fights away the darkness and not the other way around.

Before anyone in the house woke up, I left home by the main door and made my way to the Love of Crusano church. I was thinking of helping Gwendoline since she would be on church ministry to help set up the stage for the congregation. I gave no further thought about the encounter on the previous night.

I could feel pleasant presence of peace as I stepped into the church compound. It was built specially by Senior Pastor Darmor and his deceased wife about two decades ago but it remained modernized and exquisite—the product of numerous renovations which were sponsored by wealthy church members and, ahem, small donations provided by youths like myself.

The main church building was a spectacular sight even from a distance, which explained why tourists often made their way down here to catch a glimpse of its rich architecture. The ornate gates, cushioned benches, red carpets and the enormous symbol of a cyan sword on a plague hung on the wall at the front of the auditorium, made this place truly the house of a god.

And in the middle of the main hall was a great fountain. Its shimmering clear water was called Souler. It was meant for the Followers to drink from whenever they entered the church. In an old tradition from the doctrine, Crusanity believed that drinking the Souler was an act to signify your commitment to Crusano. Those who drank it half-heartedly will be bound to bad luck.

Whenever I went to church, Followers of all ages were sipping from it as if the Souler was the only essence of their life. All the other Followers were constantly reminded by the pastor and leaders to remind the other Followers to drink it before the congregation.

But I dared not drink the Souler because I was not true to the god. Yes, at the back of my head, I was clear that the Souler was merely fresh water but, I would rather keep myself on the safer side.

The church members were fervent Followers of Crusano. There were approximately five thousand plus in total. And whether or not it was true that Crusano rewards them for their faith, most of the adults there were relatively wealthy and some of them even held high social positions such as senior chief inspector of the police, district attorneys and anything that was definitely reputable in society. But since I was not a genuine Follower as I was only there to be with Gwendoline, I believed that their success had to be the results of Pastor Darmor's inspirational speeches and guidance over the years. And most certainly not some divine blessing that was claimed to be.

In today's society, education is the ignition key to drive ourselves towards a better life. Therefore, Pastor Darmor and our leaders constantly emphasized the importance of education during the sermons. He preached that Crusano needed intelligent and educated people to be his Followers to triumph over evil. Whether or not it was for Crusanity, I strongly understood that education is important. An educated person would be less ignorant towards everything in life.

As the congregation started, I sat on a bench beside Gwendoline and some of our church friends. There were two new faces—Gwendoline must have invited them to church too.

I was expecting Gwendoline to turn to me, and she did.

"Have you drunk the Souler yet?" She asked.

"Yep! What about ya?" I answered her with a lie. She nodded and told me how regenerated she felt after drinking it.

Oh come on! It is just fresh water from a tap! I would have told her this, assuming if I had the crazy guts to antagonize the whole gang of Followers around me.

I deliberately avoided that fountain of Souler whenever I passed it. I hated it if some random church fellow noticed me not drinking it. Because he would come right up to remind me, hence it made me felt awkward.

Pierre was standing on the stage with a microphone. He first shared with everyone how he was a drop-off and punk at middle school before he knew and accepted Crusano as his god. There was also a point in time when he nearly attempted a suicide. And soon, he found a purpose in life to serve Crusano and studied hard enough to enter Eropagnis college.

There were tears, cheers and claps arising from the crowd. Some people even shouted out praises to Crusano like *Crusano! The Almighty One! The purpose of our life!* While Gwendoline joined in the others and cheered, I rolled my eyes.

Oh please! Just keep what you have to say to yourself. This was neither a rock band concert nor reality television show. Besides, if I was not wrong, Crusanity doctrines mentioned that the Followers should be silent in church at all times unless permission was given to speak. To simply put it, I just disliked the raucous noise.

Silence came when Pastor Darmor took over the stage. He was a middle-aged man with a slick of white hair combed neatly to the back. He wore a black jacket with a shiny surface and it made him looked ten years younger. He was always seen smiling with his wrinkled face. His voice was deep and charismatic. All in all, he was an engaging and influential speaker who could make people listen to him and be captivated by him for hours and hours.

He chose to preach about faith today. And he brought in several examples of how some of the church members who renounced their faith, had passed away recently by tragic accidents. Although he did mention about the police investigating these cases, he made it clear that they might be the victims of demonic forces.

"The Shadow," He said. "The most dreaded servant of Avor which was known to seek victims".

I clenched my knees and trembled. I associated the horrifying figure I saw to the Shadow. What if I am its next victim? Do I really need to commit my life to Crusano in order to save myself from imminent death? But I am purely a man of science whose beliefs strictly eschewed religion!

"I vividly heard Crusano speaking to me two days ago. So I know this; we either take his blessed reward or choose the path of self-destruction." Pastor Darmor said confidently with a booming voice which set a chain of cheers that echoed through the entire church.

He is too pro-Crusanity. I thought.

Right after the sermon, Gwendoline and I went to get some refreshments before we settled down with some of the other Followers for a group session. As we sat down on a circular table in meeting room, our group leader Ronald stepped in with his ever charming smile. He was about ten years my senior with handsome chiselled features and stylish spiky hair. He greeted all of us and we responded back excitedly as if an elementary school teacher was about to start class. During such sessions, the Followers within this small group would discuss our doubts about this great god Crusano with our group leader, who was recognized to be more spiritually mature. In other words, it was religious education for us. Since Gwendoline was in it, I had to be too.

Some questions that were posted by the other Followers turned out to be very annoying and childish to me. And most infuriating, these questions were asked by young adults, not little children.

"Ronald! Can I ask why Crusano is so powerful and great?"

"Ronald! May I know why the forces of darkness crumbled under Crusano? Is it because he is too mighty?"

Oh please! They obviously knew the answers to their own questions. They were the ones cheering out loud during the sermon for Crusano after all. So they were just merely asking for the pleasure of receiving answers they were expecting; answers which advocated the greatness of Crusano. But when it was my turn to ask a question, I raised one that might be more productive. On top of that, it was a question concerning my recent horrific experience.

"With regards to the death of Followers who renounced their faith recently, do you think they should not have accepted Crusano in the first place?" I asked.

The group was silent. They were startled. Maybe this might be the first time someone actually asked a question that antagonized Crusanity. But I was sure that being critical towards this topic was vital for any improvements that should be done, because if everyone had the same point of view, then it would get us nowhere.

Ronald flashed a quick smile at me and looked through his files.

I hope he better give me a good answer to that!

Then, he turned to me with an answer.

"Koby. Crusano is the god that controls the world. According to chapter nine of the doctrine, it was said that there will be a day when the forces of evil will wage war and claim all souls to an eternal damnation. Only the Followers will remain in the world." Ronald replied. "Therefore, those who do not even accept Crusano in the first place will eventually suffer."

I hated it whenever people supported their arguments with religious doctrines. I want a clear and logical explanation that could be justified with actual facts and not religious accounts with no solid evidence. But nevertheless, I nodded my head and thanked Ronald.

"Nice one Kob!" Gwendoline nudged me from the side and shot a wink. I hoped she was not praising me for giving Ronald another opportunity to advocate the might of Crusano. I wanted her to praise me for bringing up a valid point.

I helped with cleaning up the meeting room after the session. I took a wet cloth and wiped the table whereas the other Followers mopped the floor, scrubbed the mirrors and brushed the chairs. Then Pierre and Gwendoline came up to me.

"That night at the cafe, you said you saw something. Well, Pierre actually had the same experience. You should speak with him." Gwendoline told me. I was guessing that she might have picked up a hint that I was not behaving like usual ever since the night at Chopper's Café.

"So what did you see?" I asked Pierre.

"Like one week ago, I actually saw this dark shadow following me when I returned home late during the night," Pierre recounted. "I was like so scared because of the deaths of the backsliders . . ."

Before he even continued, I knew he was somehow going to integrate Crusano's divine protection into his experience. And I was right.

"Then I prayed to Crusano like what Pastor Darmor told us to do and the shadowy thing disappears!" Pierre exclaimed.

That's it! I had enough of this nonsense. Crusano! Crusano! Crusano! Why is everything about him?

I let out an angry growl which got the attention of everyone in that room. Even if I did not lose my insanity to that ghostly stalker, I was sure to lose it to this bunch of people!

"Kob please chill! Pierre is just encouraging you." Gwendoline patted my shoulder while she tried to cool me down. Unfortunately, Pierre was not as accommodating.

"Crusano gave me hope in life when I couldn't find any. He taught me how to be a better person!" Pierre argued back rebelliously, somewhat showing his punk nature from before.

"It is just Pastor Darmor who made you a better person through his teachings," I argued confrontationally. "If Crusnao is really magnanimous, why didn't he just protect those people?"

"He is just a petty and selfish god! Or in fact, he doesn't exist!' I snapped.

"Kob! How can you even say that?" Gwendoline chided me. I regretted my actions. I should have known that Gwendoline hated people who insult her faith.

I ran out from the room and out of church with tears streaming down my cheeks. Is this really the price to pay for liking Gwendoline? I came to church because of her. I forced myself to be a Follower because of her. And now, I made contact with the spiritual world in which I was not ready to confront its horror. But she only treated me as nothing more than a friend. *I wanted to be a more important person to her.*

I was constantly irritated by people's immaturity, and ironically, I turned out to be the most childish.

I took a cab to the nearest bar. I needed the leisure of a good drink and some loud music. Besides, Barbara's bar would be flooded with many people during the evening, where the atmosphere would be the most enjoyable. I wanted to brighten up my mood.

True enough, my head felt lighter when I took a couple of strong alcoholic apple juice and watched the other patrons dancing along the rock music. A scantily dressed young lady stepped beside me and offered for a dance. I declined. Gwendoline was on my mind. No other ladies could replace her in my heart.

When I felt a little dizzy from the alcohol, I left the place and made my way home on foot since the distance was not far. I initially wanted to take a cab home but the visit to the bar had sucked my pockets dry. In addition, catching a little night breeze might be comforting.

The streets were empty. Most citizens of Eropagnis ought to be sleeping right now. I must have been in the bar for hours! Time fly fast whenever I am enjoying myself.

My legs felt as though they were in iron casings when I took every step. My vision was clouded and my stomach felt bloated—the toll for drinking too much.

Then, I saw it again.

The ghost stalker.

It was behind a fence near the alleyway. It was glaring at me through the metal grilles.

During that instant, how I wished I was not drunk so that I could confirm its presence rather than being deceived by my own imagination. Yet, my drunken state gave me a newfound power against this treacherous foe. This power was widely known as Dutch courage.

I lifted up a broad wooden plank from a nearby trash can and I dashed straight at the stalker. I let out a fearsome war cry as if I was some kind of champion from a nomadic tribe. *It is do or die.* I swore to myself.

I ruggedly climbed over the fence and landed on boxes of unwanted cardboard with my eyes fiercely fixed on the ghost. I charged at it and brandishing the wooden plank like a great sword. My "sword" swung so hard that I could almost hear the whistling sound of it slicing through the air, even the greatest foe will crumble under this strike.

The shadowy figure stumbled backwards for a second. It darted its head out from under its shrouded hood and blasted a shriek.

A pale white face, yellow huge eyes and razor sharp fangs for its teeth. It looked exactly like the demon from my dreams.

I gasped. A tingle ran up my spine. My whole body froze. I dropped my weapon. I was defenceless. I was speechless.

It was dressed in a black robe. It was not a ghost. It looked like a vampire, but no. It was a demon described in Crusanity doctrines.

The Shadow demon.

"Leave the unblessed cyan sword or you will face a fate more terrible than eternal damnation." It hissed dangerously. I was amazed that it could speak.

"Wh . . . What do you mean?" I asked, trying hard not to express any signs of weaknesses.

It remained silent as it covered its face with the black hood. Darkness conjured around it. It seemed like the demon summoned the darkness. Within seconds, it faded away into the shadows, hissing as it moved out of sight.

I stayed motionless and rigid before I collapsed hard onto the ground, knees down first, then the upper body and face. Exhaustion crept up my muscle system, fear overwhelmed my nervous system and confusion infected my mental system. The encounter was not my imagination.

I saw it with my own eyes and even heard its monstrous voice.

I laid down on the cold ground, breathless while staring into the starless night sky above me. After resting for half an hour or so, I managed to regain my composure. I began thinking about that thing; what it was trying to tell me and why did it not hurt or kill me when it had the chance.

A glimmer from my wrist caught my attention. It was emitted from my watch, the one with the unique design which I treasured the most.

Wait. That should be it! I thought.

The symbol of Crusano, the cyan sword must have prevented me from harm! I felt rather awkward coming up with this conclusion since I was not the religious or superstitious sort. The thought of a watch as talisman felt absolutely ridiculous. Well, but I have to admit that there will be a point where a person will bound to give supernatural reasons, especially when a situation seem to be unexplainable.

And I wondered what it was telling me. Leave the unblessed cyan sword? Was it referring to my watch with the cyan sword? That vile demon might be threatening me to remove my only "protection" against it. And I am sure glad I was not gullible enough to do that.

I knew I had offended that demon by foiling its attempt to harm me. I even put up a resistance. I was sure it will come back to exact its revenge on me. Or even my loved ones. I had to something about it and put an end to it. It was too real to be ignored.

Should I go to church and seek advice from Pastor Darmor or Ronald? No I should not. They would just tell me to stay faithful to Crusano, pray genuinely and continue to commit my life to him. Even by doing so, I was sure it would take more than just heart-felt prayers to rid this threat.

To me, a prayer was nothing more than a mental conviction towards oneself, to convince the mind that everything will be fine. Although it did offered hope, assurance and peace, drastic actions had to be done in my situation.

Jack! The self-proclaimed extreme ghost buster and demon trapper came to my mind. If that demon could exist in a scientific world, I was sure that scientific measures might work. I hated to say, but he was the only option left for me because I did not know when the demon might strike at me again. And this time, it would strike harder.

Much harder. I was completely sure.

And I must get ready for it.

The next day at college, I ignored Gwendoline. After losing my temper at Pierre yesterday, I could not face her. After all, the Followers were expected to control their anger, but I failed to do so. Most regretfully, I caused her to be upset

Then immediately after class, I went straight up to Jack. He was picking his nose but as soon as he realized that I was approaching him, he put his finger away and attempted to tidy his facial hair. He stood up and cleared his throat as if he was about to give a prestigious speech.

"What brings Koby Sleuth here?" He asked. I sensed he was trying to cover his excitement over this potential customer.

"I need your help Jack. Please." I told him politely.

His facial expression changed. His droopy eyes became sharp and his body muscles tightened. It was clear to him that I was not here for help in physics.

"Alright. Come over to Jack's house at eight tonight," He said with a pretentious deep manly voice. Then, he went back to his original voice of a higher pitch. "But don't forget to bring at least one hundred dollars for my service!"

I smiled.

THE GUY NAMED JACK

JACK LIVED IN a small apartment room in Westside of Eropagnis city. The apartment block was a dull grey tall building with dirt patches all over the walls. It was definitely not an ideal place to stay.

During the evening as I crossed the streets in Westside, I saw street gangsters hanging around the pathways. When some of them spotted me, they were calling out to me, with the intention to make youngsters like myself a part of their gang. The Central Eropagnis Police Bureau made tremendous effort to clear up crime over the past few years, unfortunately, Westside was the only part of the city they neglected—it was not worth the while due to the presence of too many impoverished citizens in that area.

I pressed the squishy button beside the door. There was no sound.

I pressed it harder. Still silent.

I pressed it even harder and finally, a loud beep was heard. The front door sprang opened and Jack was there. His face and shirt were greasy, and he was holding a screwdriver in one of his hand and a spanner in the other.

"Welcome to Jack's humble home!" He invited me into his house as he rubbed his backhand on his face to wipe off the grease. When I stepped into the house, my right foot sank into a puddle of black liquid. Thankfully, my shoe was on.

Jack's apartment represented a miniaturized workshop, a mad scientist's lair or, a junkyard. There were workbenches, metal tools, gizmos, books and everything scattered everywhere and anywhere. Jack could not have afforded all these; hence it might be scavenged from unwanted trash. Worst of all, little creepy crawlers were treated the messy place like a playground.

"Okay! How can Jack help you sir?" Jack formally asked. The way he said "sir" reminded me of a salesman who worked at a departmental store down the street. Anyway, so I explained my frightening encounters to Jack and sought his advice.

"Alright Jack understands. But first . . ." Jack opened his palm towards me. I slapped a hundred dollar bill into it. He continued. "What you are dealing with might be a high level demon which can materialize its physical form to harm humans."

"Get to point Jack. I want to know how to stop it." I told him off impatiently. I felt heart-broken for giving away that hundred dollar bill.

"The Exlecutor. You need the Exlecutor." He reached out into a nearby drawer and drew a tiny round flat piece of metal. It was around the size of my palm with dozens of electrical circuits on it.

"So this is the Exlecutor? A mini disc?"

"Yes! Yes! Yes! This cutting edge technology will stun all demons!" Jack explained. "Flick this switch and throw it at that monster!"

That sounded a little too easy to be true.

"Stun it? I want to get rid of it!" I demanded.

"One step at a time. In order to get rid of it, just take a dagger and plunge its heart," Jack sounded confident. "Jack is going to watch over you stealthily and when that thing appears, we kill it!"

The word *kill* stunned me. I have never killed anyone before. But then again, I would be killing a demon, not a person. Surely that should not be considered a crime. In fact, I ought to receive a medal of good citizenry for getting rid of this threat!

"Mission one initiates tonight. Hang around the dark and deserted places to lure the target out!" Jack commanded.

I placed the Exlecutor in my side pocket and Jack sheathed his dagger. As he left his apartment, I caught a glimpse of a series of books littered on the ground. They were famous fictional novels about demon hunters and that sort of paranormal thing. These were best-selling stories that kept sci-fi fans addicted for hours.

I sure hope Jack knows what he is doing.

Black.

It was the color of the night sky. Under the luminous shine of the moonlight, I ambled towards the city's central graveyard. Its morbid atmosphere was the best location for the demon to surface itself, according to Jack of course.

I wished there were no wandering ghosts which might unknowingly disrupt our operation. Jack followed closely behind me from a distance. We could not risk spooking the demon away without killing it.

I sat beside a tombstone and waited. I heard my heartbeat pounding under the silence of the graveyard. My right hand sweated as I stuffed it into my pocket, grasping the Exlecutor and getting ready to throw it at a moment's notice.

I breathed heavily. I did not from which direction it will emerge.

From behind the tombstone I am looking at? From below the ground like a rising zombie? Or from above?

My head remained motionless, yet my eyes darted around everywhere.

I have to spot it before it gets a chance to touch me.

Hours and hours passed. Only the endless hoots from the owls were heard. I stood up and walked towards Jack. I decided to call it a night.

"That thing must have sensed our trap!" Jack exploded.

I was not angry. Instead, I was actually quite relieved. At least, I could live to see tomorrow. But I did not put this to a rest.

"We will do this again tomorrow night. I won't give up. Neither will you right?"

For the next two nights, we camped at the graveyard. I simply told Aunt Joan that I was staying over at a friend's place. I reluctantly paid Jack a hundred dollar for every night as he requested. No discounts were given.

Jack brought most of the camping equipments; tents, kerosene lamps, sleeping bags, canned food and bottles of water. I only brought the Exlecutor. To me, stopping that creature was all that matters.

Unfortunately, even after the two sleepless nights, there was no catch. Technically, I should consider it to be two peaceful and undisturbed nights. And we finally gave up our stay at the graveyard. I still had the bad feeling that Jack was behind everything.

Back in college, I hung out with Jack more than I did with Gwendoline. Although I was still in love her, I understood that she had a own social circle to mingle with. Besides, it would be annoying on her side if I was constantly sticking to her. Perhaps, this period was an opportunity to provide the both of us with some space.

In the morning, our engineering class received the grades for our first national exam which was done at the beginning of the year. The second, third and final exams would commence at the end of the year. The cumulative score of all the exams will decide our chances for university admission. Jack came in top again, whereas I did pass well enough.

I was not sure about Gwendoline's grade but I was sure she made it too. And next, it was Pierre. He failed the exam.

Whoever failed this exam ought to leave the National College of Eropagnis. While the other students who failed wept in tears of sorrow and regrets as they bade farewell to other students, Pierre was strong-headed and happy.

"It is okay! My great Crusano is planning a greater purpose for us!" Pierre cheered.

He is badly disillusioned. I thought.

You can call it optimism. Yet to me, it was a loser's excuse. I mean how can we bring in religious reasoning just to justify our own failure?

The majority of Pierre's time spent at church ministry could be used for productive revisions. I sensed that I cared for his future nonetheless.

The school cafeteria was crowded during the afternoon. I waved to Jack who was carrying a tray of mash potatoes and fries. His eyebrows raised and he cut his way through the other people towards my table. Then, he took a sit and offered me some of his food. I laughed and scooped some of it on my plate.

"Look, Koby and Jack are together as an item." Students passing by were giggling at us. I recognized them to be members of the Love of Crusano church too. I was disappointed in them. The Followers ought to condemn badmouthing and yet, they were outrightly violating that principle.

So what? They are *part-time Followers?* I smirked and shook my head. *They were pretending to be holy in church. A bunch of hypocrites.*

Unlike back in middle school when I tend to overreact to other people's scornful remarks, I ignored them. I did not see the reason as to why I should get worked up over such comments which don't affect my life.

At the same time, I could not blame them entirely for saying things like that. Being eccentric or some defined as crazy, Jack had no friends in college to hang out with. There were only two situations where he was seen interacting with others; firstly was when Jack promoted his paranormal services. And secondly was when students asked him to teach them physics or math. It was indeed expected that people will make conclusions about our relationship.

I looked at Gwendoline who was sitted at a distance away amongst her group of girlfriends. She barely noticed me. And when one of her friends spotted me, I quickly turned away.

"Oh yeah! You once told Jack that the Shadow spoke to you before. What did it say?" said Jack, who was barely inaudible with the chunks of food churning in his mouth.

"Hmm . . . it told me to leave the unblessed cyan sword or I will face a fate more terrible than eternal damnation," I recounted. "Might be a riddle?"

Jack firmly planted his elbow on the table and propped his head up. His fingers stroked his chin and he scowled. He was giving the impression of processing intelligent thoughts.

"The cyan sword definitely refers to the Crusanity religion or that god Crusano himself," Jack deduced. "Jack thinks it was threatening you to renounce your faith from Crusanity so that it will not harm you."

"What? That's it? This was exactly its hidden intention! It was trying to trick me to give up on Crusano so that I will be defenceless against it!" I rebuked.

"And you once mentioned that you are not religious. Then why fear denying divine protection?" Jack got me. I was caught speechless. Deep down beneath my egoistical nature, I knew I needed some divine help.

Suddenly, Jack's eyes brightened.

"Jack thinks the key to this riddle might be the term *unblessed cyan sword*." He pointed out.

"Unblessed cyan sword? Does that mean unblessed . . . Crusanity?" I asked curiously.

Jack nodded.

Although I did not understand what that meant, Jack suggested that I should come over to his house after school to do a research. He claimed to have an artificial intelligent system known as BRAIN (Brilliant Robotic Artificially Intelligent Navigator), which may answer all our questions.

I was not sure how it worked but Jack made it sound most impressive. Or he might be over exaggerating the ability of an ordinary computer by coming up with such a fanciful name for it.

If he really possessed such state-of-the-art technology, I was also wondering how he could afford it in his impoverished state. Wait, it might be the money from the fees I paid for his services the nights before, assuming that three hundred dollars in total was sufficed to purchase it. If not, he could have built it out of scratch from the trash he collected. Although it felt almost impossible to me.

But still, I was indeed looking forward to meet this BRAIN. Most significantly, I was looking forward to put an end to this nightmarish experience. As a pre-emptive measure, I stayed alert and wary. I seemed to realize the demon was not seen for the past few days ever since Jack became my friend . . .

BRAIN

I MADE MY way through the maze of metal junks lying everywhere on the ground towards Jack who sat beside a rectangular machine, a resemblance to a printer. Fortunately, it did not turn out to be a computer. He fiddled with some controls on that machine and told me to wait before the system could be recalibrated.

There were sounds of car engine ignition and gears cracking against each other. The machine roared to life as Jack gave a child-like squeal.

"Greetings I am BRAIN," The artificial intelligence introduced itself through a monotonous and metallic voice that emitted through the speakers. "I'm also known as Brilliant Robotic Artificially Intelligent Navigator. I will lead you onto the right path for all your human doubts . . ."

"Cut the crap! Password nine two three. Skip the introduction!" Jack interrupted. BRAIN turned silent as if a dog was obediently obeying its master.

"Is this thing reliable?" I critiqued. Jack did not answer my question—he wanted to show me the answer.

"Alright Koby. Ask BRAIN a question. As difficult as possible. Use specific and clear keywords to avoid ambiguity." Jack prompted me. So I asked a question that stumbled most students during an extra philosophy lesson which I attended in college.

"BRAIN, if the pen is mightier than the sword, then why does action speak louder than words?" I was expecting an irrelevant answer or a syntax error, but I was wrong.

"Your question involves philosophy. Philosophies are merely ideologies that are perceived differently by different people." BRAIN thoroughly answered. "Hence, the two sayings that you have mentioned are no doubt originated from two different persons who experienced their lives differently. Thus, they came up with different perspectives."

My jaws dropped. I was dumbfounded—too deeply amazed by such technologically marvel. I was first impressed by how it understood my verbal language and secondly, most impressed by its ability to provide answers of logical reasoning, as if it was indeed a human, or I should say, a very smart human.

Then I turned my attention to BRAIN's inventor, Jack. I could not even express how super ingenious he was. A top student, a good friend and now, a brilliant inventor. I had to admit my admiration towards him.

"Dude! How does it work?" I asked in bemusement.

He told me that BRAIN's system was programmed to link up to all the infinite information on the internet and all the information would be synthesized to derive the most logical answer. He included explaining the feature that allows BRAIN to be portable.

"Impressive huh? Now BRAIN, define the term *unblessed cyan sword* from Crusanity." The both of us listened closely.

"Your question involves Crusanity religion. The cyan sword is symbol for this religion. So an unblessed cyan sword means . . ." I swallowed a ball of phlegm down my throat and listened hard.

". . . the religion itself is unholy, wicked or bad." BRAIN concluded.

So that stalking demon was telling me Crusanity is in fact unholy, wicked and bad? Of course it will say that! It was common sense for a demon to detest Crusanity! I immediately felt that this had become a wild goose chase. Then I asked another question that had been burning inside me and many other people for millenniums.

"BRAIN. Do gods exist? I asked.

Jack threw up a thumbs-up.

"Your question involves cosmology. Yes, gods exist. Or I should say god exists. Since the formation of this world is too perfect for it to be caused by just nothing!" BRAIN answered.

"BRAIN, then is Crusano real?" I pursued further.

"Your question linked to the previous. Yes, Crusano and other gods from religions are real. But they are in fact the same omnipotent entity who appeared in the different forms in the eyes of man."

"So how can I connect to this living divine entity?" I questioned.

"Your question linked to the previous. The omnipotent being can only be contacted within your own heart. It can be felt as the human conscience. If man forgets about it, it will no longer exist to us."

BRAIN spoke the logical truth. The human conscience is the founding father of all spiritual guidance. Religions are initiated by man's innate ability to differentiate the right from wrong. The almighty omnipotent being made us that way. Crusano was merely a way Followers interpreted and portrayed this logic, similar to how Kanaism, Vitulo and all other religions perceived the human conscience.

On top of that, now I did understand why people who served the same god deserved different blessings, and some no blessings at all. Not because the almighty one out there was being biased, but rather the difference of how each individual connects to it.

With this connection known as the human conscience, the only and greatest blessing we might receive would be our personality. If we connect to this "god" with the correct human conscience, we will be hardworking, thrifty and honest—virtues that allow us to live as a more successful or better person. The wrong connection will doom us with a life of self-deceit and eventually, failure. To simply put it, the god can only be found by ourselves.

I went into deep insightful thoughts and I had one final question for BRAIN.

"BRAIN, do demons really exist?"

"Your question involves the arcane . . ." Before BRAIN could give an answer, Jack clicked on several buttons and intervened.

"Okay. Sorry no more questions. Jack wants to test its security system now." Jack apologized. I got pissed. Was that intentional? If so, why did he do that?

BRAIN's terminal glowed green. Jack explained that he had rigged up a perimeter tracker that can detect any person within a radius of five meters. He mentioned that it would glow bright red if the sensor detected unfamiliar people within the radius.

Speak of devil. Our breaths stopped when the terminal glowed red.

"What does this mean?" I asked to seek clarification.

"Jack made it clear. This means there is someone else in Jack's humble home other than the two of us." he replied.

We spun around to catch a sight on the unknown third party. There was nothing except the metallic parts that were littered around.

The main moth-eaten door swung back and forth along the flowing wind which howled its way in. Somebody or something opened it. I swore I locked the door tight after I came in!

Immediately, a patch of darkness zoomed out towards the front door. The demon once again reared its ugly head. I was no longer afraid, because I had the means to defend myself and destroy it.

I ran closer to the hooded demon. With lightning fast reflex, I drew out the Exlecutor from my side pocket. I doubted neither Jack's technology nor his intentions anymore after the Q and A session with the spectacular BRAIN, plus the demon was definitely not Jack in disguise.

Upon flicking the switch on the Exlecutor, bolts of crackling blue electricity raced through the device's circuit. And before, the demon could even reach the front door. I flung the electrically charged disc at it. With unerring accuracy, the weapon met its mark.

The Exlecutor attached itself onto the demon's right leg while a blast of electricity surged up to its body. It shrieked in unbearable pain and agony before it lost its footing and crashed into the pile of metallic tools lying on the ground.

It was stunned. This time was for Jack to end this game.

A dagger in hand, Jack leaped towards the downed adversary to prepare the final blow. He wielded the blade into position like an experienced demon hunter from fictional films. The demon retaliated by sweeping Jack across his face with its arm. Jack was knocked off balanced and he tripped over a pool of steel ball bearings on the ground. He landed like a bull in a china shop.

The demon regained its footing. I saw its facial features again and it was as frightening as before. When it opened its mouth to reveal a set of razor sharp teeth, to my horror, I thought it was about to deliver a lethal bite on Jack. But it did not. Instead it dashed out of the front door and attempting to escape.

"Don't just stand there! Go after it! It might be our only chance!" Jack called out and hurled a new weapon, which he pulled out from under a table, into my grasp. "Behold! The Nettingale!"

The word sounded like Nightingale, Gwendoline's family name. And I started thinking about Gwendoline Nightingale as I ran out of the front door to pursue that creature. I was thinking as to what Gwendoline would do if she was in my position. Would she risk her life to rid the demon for the better good of others? Or would she stop pursuing and keep safe? But I'd came this far, and there was no turning back for me.

I cornered the demon at the end of the gloomy and empty corridors. Under the flickering bulbs that faintly lit my vision, I fixed my eyes on its malevolent yellow eyes. I could not afford to blink as I was worried that it might just vanish away under the cover of flickering lights in a split second.

I aimed the Nettingale weapon at it like a rifle. As a matter of fact, the Nettingale was indeed shaped like an air rifle with exotic pipes linking the components together. I pulled the trigger, there was a loud bang and a heavy net of steel mesh blasted out from the front nozzle.

The impact from the net forced the target to slam backwards against the cemented wall. The demon shrugged off the steel mesh with ease despite the weight off it. I cursed when the net failed to incapacitate the foe.

I must hold it down until Jack catches up. He has the dagger! I told myself. I lunged forward and speared the demon with all my might.

I thought I would be ripped into pieces by its demonic strength. And intriguingly, I physically put up quite a good wrestle as I tightly held on to its black robes. Blistered were popping out from my fingers. It then lifted me off the ground by a grapple and I came face to face with it.

Despite the monstrous face twisted into a ferocious expression, the facial features were noticeably that of a female.

It was a female demon.

She tossed me to the ground and jumped on top my body. My collar was grabbed by her claw-like hands that sprung out from her robe's long sleeves. But she was not strangling my throat.

"I told you to leave the Crusano church or you will suffer!" She hissed.

I knew I was about to die. The Crusanity designed watch was no longer my protective talisman. Or perhaps it was not even a protective talisman in the first place.

There was a thud. The demon fell onto me and I pushed my palms against the ground to jerk back away from her.

There was a bolo wrapped around her arms and torso. The wires were too tight for the demon to set free.

Another thud came. A second bolo rapidly tied itself around her ankles. She was finally incapacitated.

It took me a few seconds to regain my breath before I was able to look up. Jack was strolling towards my direction and he was casually spinning another bolo in the air with his right hand.

"Jack scores!" He smiled at me and looked at the bounded demon struggling and rolling on the ground. "Can we keep it?."

I disagreed with him. The demons are not pets.

I wanted the demon dead, or I should say it was too dangerous to be kept alive. But then, I wanted to find out more about its origin and whether it might the only one.

"Okay. We'll keep it for now," I nodded. "We need to lock it up well, very well."

I hoped curiosity does not kill the cat.

Demon Revealed

It required the combined strength of Jack and me to drag the demon along the corridor. Jack's apartment was the ideal place to lock her up; it was near and on top of that, Jack claimed to have a ghost trapping cage in his storeroom, and maybe, it might work on demons too. She had flesh just like anyone else. I was just afraid that it might bite either one of us with its fangs without any warning.

"Too bad for it! The demon tried to stalk you and now we got it! Jack got it!" Jack commented.

"Enough! Enough! I am not the Shadow! Let me go you rascals!" she wailed. Jack and I released our hands on her robes. Her voice was different. Not eerie or monstrous anymore, it sounded just like a normal person.

She chewed on something and spitted it out. I initially thought it was dangerous such as a ball of corrosive acid or a tiny diabolical demon spawn. But it was not. Instead, it was a set of fangs. Then, she tugged one of her sharp finger pointed hands with the other and yanked it really hard. The claws came right off. And she did the same on the other hand. No more large demonic claws. Only small tender human hands were seen.

"Holy! You are a human!" Jack was startled as much as I was.

Jack sat on a table while I tried to pack up some of his spare tools lying all around his room. The both of us remained silent as we waited anxiously for the "demon" to wash her face in the bathroom. We would demand an explanation when she comes out.

I was confused. Why did she dress herself up as a demon and try to harm me? Why did she murder those people who left church?

"Jack, it appears that demons don't exist. Only mad people do." I broke the awkward silence.

"Demons do exist! It is just not this one!" Jack rebuked in anger. He might have got the wrong message. I was not referring him as a mad person, but rather I was referring to the "demon". Alright, basically he was angry as I once again doubted the existence of the supernatural.

I apologized. He looked away.

The "demon" walked out of the bathroom. She carried her demonic black robes over her shoulder and used a towel to dry her neck-length brown hair.

"Now that I have washed off that whitish face paint and removed those yellow contact lenses. I'll get straight to the point." She said in a brash tone.

"Who are you and why in the world did you do that? Is scaring people that fun?" I shouted in her face.

"The name's Paige. I resorted to do this in order to scare you and people away from the Love of Crusano church." Paige replied. She was tall, slim and fair. Judging from her facial features, she ought to be in her early twenties and quite beautiful. Her name was familiar to me but I just could not recall where and when it was heard. Her face looked just as familiar.

"Why did you do that? And why did you murder some of those people who left church?" I bombarded her with questions. Jack gave a nonchalant look—I doubt he understood anything that we were saying since he was not a member of our church.

"Well, I did scare people, including your friend Pierre. But I did not physically hurt anyone, neither was I responsible for the deaths of those church backsliders." She explained confidently. "Pastor Darmor and church leaders . . . are responsible."

My eyes widen and urged her to elaborate. What did she mean by Pastor Darmor and church leaders being responsible for the deaths of the Followers?

"Darmor is working on a plan to make a new generation of Followers," Paige continued. "This new generation will heed his every order. He wants to a king."

"How's that possible?" I questioned. It was impossible for him to be that dominating with municipal laws and governments in place.

"In the future, there will be tons of wealthy, powerful, intelligent people under his influence. He'll use the less competent ones for his dirty work. Countless of people will support and vote for him with if he wants to enter politics."

"So that's why he is always telling church members to bring new friends to church to get to know the god Crusano!" I blurted. All that goodness from Pastor Darmor was ultimately for his own benefit. I was utterly disappointed.

She then moved on to explain the reason behind the deaths of the back-sliders. I gasped in disbelieve.

"Darmor called a hit on them for leaving the church and leaving his influence. He just wants to deceivingly show what happens to people who so-called decline Crusano's protection. It's all his bullshit!" She raised her voice and clenched her fist.

I understood everything now. Paige pretended to be the Shadow demon to frighten church members away from church because she knew Darmor's diabolical plan. Yet, Darmor twisted the situation to his favor by making it seemed as though death was the price of their renounced faith. Therefore, it kept the disillusioned Followers even closer to their blind faith.

"We have to call the cops. He is committing contract murder!" I needed to seek justice for the victims and, the potential victims of this conspiracy.

I lifted up my phone and prepared to dial. But my heart sank when Paige said there was no evidence.

"How did you even know so much?" Jack, who was silent for so long, started asking.

She sighed.

"I was Darmor's wife." She revealed. But everyone at church thought she'd passed away six years ago from cancer.

"I knew of his plans six years ago and he wanted me to be a part of it. But I couldn't live with myself if I am benefitting myself in the name of a god."

Tears flowed down her eyes like waterfall that started from a mere tickle of water. She sobbed hysterically and continued.

"He was a changed man, consumed by ambitious, greed and cruelty! He feared that I will reveal his plan so, he tried to kill me—forced me to drink a specially designed unique chemical that instantly causes fatal cancer." She recalled. Her fists were tight and vibrating.

"Wow! That pastor guy can make a poison that instantly gives someone cancer?" Jack interrupted. "That's like the best way to assassinate someone!"

According to what I heard from some of church members, Pastor Darmor was once a brilliant chemist before he became pastor. Hence, this information did not surprise me.

"But of course, his chemical failed," She moved on explaining her youthful appearance just when I was comparing Darmor's age to hers. "Instead of causing an abnormal cell growth which leads to death, it allowed cells and tissues constantly regenerate."

"Then where have you been all these years?"

"Aside from the little café I am managing, I was hiding and observing the Followers of the church. Until recently, I knew I had to do something. Since no one will believe me, I resorted to scare tactics." Paige scowled. "Fear might be the best method to get things done."

"Looks like your efforts might be in vain. Because of your little trick, some of them increased their conviction towards to church," I sighed. My friend Pierre was clearly one of these people. And maybe even other Followers whom she attempted to frighten. "But since we do not have any evidence, I'm afraid . . ."

"We do! Darmor does! I sure of it! He has the habit to keep documents in his house." Paige swept her loose fringe back.

"Oh how do we get it then?" Jack asked sarcastically.

"Sneak into his house! I couldn't do it alone as there are security systems I couldn't breach." Paige became excited and she wept her dried tears away. She might had had this idea for a very long time. "Cameras, alarms, guard dogs and who knows what."

"Koby and Jack could deal with that!" Jack winked at her with assurance. I frowned—I did not even agree for this trespassing thing and yet, Jack just signed up for me? Besides, I thought Jack was only interested in demon hunting, who knew he actually found this to be quite appealing. I folded my arms and stared at him.

"Thank you! Thank you! I hope Darmor will learn from his mistake by the hands of the law." Paige burst into tears again, but now, they were tears of joy and hope. I could sense she still loved her husband a lot. She was determined to set him on the right path again. My heart melted, I wanted to help her.

"Right then. We shall strike the day after tomorrow in the afternoon. Darmor will be out at church for the leaders meeting then." I said, according to some of the church updates I received.

"In the afternoon? Then what about school?" Jack obviously knew the answer.

"We skip it. But you must remember to coach me in all subjects when this top-secret agent mission is completed yea?" I told him. The three of us went into laughter.

School was getting much more tensed than before, the curriculums in all the classes were increasing difficult—more complex concepts, more demanding grading system and much more stricter teachers. But with the assistance Jack and his A.I. BRAIN, learning had never been so easy.

After the last lesson that evening, I went to the arcade and gamed. The place was a haunting spot for a lot of youths like me. The atmosphere was filled with electronic noises and colorful lights from the dozens of game consoles. My favorite game was boxing, since I could virtually beat up some random person to unleash my rage. I needed to get my mind focused on something else, instead of constant thoughts of how despicable that pastor was.

After knocking out a muscular opponent from the game, I went to the vending machine to purchase a soda. Two people walked right passed me when I bent down to pick the can from the dispenser. I stood up and took a look at them.

One of them was Gwendoline. I was curiously amused. With her type of personality, she certainly was not a gamer. Maybe she just came with her friend. I looked at her friend. It was our church leader Ronald.

And they were holding hands. Their fingers crossed over each other's.

I stood there motionless as my heart broke. I was devastated. It was obviously clear that they were together, even an idiot could tell.

Gwendoline's beauty, charm and personality made her a favor to men. I was aware that a lot of guys in church and class liked her. She rejected all of them and now, she chose the best of them all; Ronald was handsome, charming and wise. For that very moment, jealously seduced me. I tried very hard to resist it. I wished not to be morally flawed like Darmor since jealously could lead me down on that path.

I understood that relationships could not be force upon by anyone—it must be a two-sided feeling. Wait. Was it because I failed to be upfront about my feelings towards her? No! Even if I did that, I was sure to be rejected like dozens of other guys who tried before.

My eyes felt a little wet and took a deep breath. I reminded myself to be more mature and to see things with an open mind.

She has the right to choose for herself. As a friend, I must respect her decision.

Then I thought of the important mission that I would be undergoing the next day, in order to feel good about myself. If I could expose the evil behind Darmor's masquerade of holiness, then Gwendoline, Ronald and everyone else would be grateful to me.

No. I should never think like that. I am doing it out of goodwill. I am doing this for the rightful justice to the people who were murdered by that pastor, and to seek justice for their grieving families. Not for personal pride.

As Gwendoline and Ronald were happily playing at a game station, I strolled out of the arcade and anticipated on strategies to sneak enter Darmor's house to find the evidence.

Any mistake means that I might have a trespasser or burglar criminal record for the rest of my life. I will be expelled from college. Aunt Joan will be disappointed with me. Gwendoline will despise me. Worst of all, Darmor will get away with his crime.

"Any true god out there, either be it Crusano or something else, if you can hear me, bless us with a smooth mission tomorrow." I prayed. I just needed some hope and assurance for the oncoming death trap.

The most genuine and sincere prayer I had ever made in my entire life. Surprisingly, it felt good.

TRESPASSER

THE ARROWS OF rain clashed onto the earth of Eropagnis city. The skies were deep grey as the sunlight was consumed by an enormous wave of darkening cloud. I wore a simple T-shirt and jeans. Paige came in a navy blue track jacket. And Jack, ahem, he was suited up in a black skin suit with a pair of goggles, resembling a special-ops agent literally. But at least he was dressed in a much less exaggerated manner than I expected him to.

The three of us crouched down under the cover of a thick bush behind Pastor Darmor's house. He lived in a multi-storey mansion. There was a large garden in the front yard with a Jacuzzi, and the fine sculpture of majestic pillars and stairways at the main door boasted his vast wealth.

"I thought Darmor lives in church?" I turned to Paige.

She told me it was merely a false impression to appear humble to the other Followers. She elaborated that the money he embezzled from church funds along with the savings from his earlier days as a chemist, made him a multi-billionaire.

"Rich he is. Now he just wanted power to dominate people." Paige said, while Jack's saliva was still dripping from his mouth as he stared at the mansion's exterior in awe.

Paige stated that the evidence might be located within Darmor's computer in the study room. All we needed was to get to rear door of the house, throw a grappling hook onto the ledge of the window, and then move into the study room's window. This might save us the trouble of avoiding security cameras and alarms which guarded the main living room and corridors.

Paige vaulted over the high walls with spectacular agility. It was fast, silent and efficient—she appeared blurring in motion. Now I understood how she managed to pull off several gravity defying stunts that scared me when she pretended to be a demon.

"Just a few little tricks I picked from gymnastics in high school." She beamed and reached out her hands to help pull Jack and me up.

We landed softly onto a patch of grass in the front garden and surreptitiously made our way to the rear door by moving along the boundaries of the mansion.

Low and dangerous growls stopped us in our tracks. There were three guards blocking our path and showing their teeth in aggression.

Rottweilers.

"Jack knows doggies like sticks. Let's pick that branch and throw it." Jack suggested.

Paige carefully waved her hand.

"Nicole, Ling and Karn. You have no business here. Go back to your kennels." She ordered.

The three ferocious large dogs wagged their tails. They yelped and complied. The path was clear.

"Wow! You know them?" I curiously asked.

"They're still little puppies when I first bought them. I can't believe how big they are now." Paige was not answering my question directly but I knew the answer.

"Err . . . Paige. Did you buy that too? Jack thinks you need a refund." Jack tapped our shoulders. We turned our heads to his direction.

There was a black leonine beast standing beside the Jacuzzi. It glared at us hungrily and breathed heavily, salivating. It stood on two limbs, and the other two were arms with crude claws and brute muscles.

"What is that? A werewolf?" I badly wanted an answer on this thing.

"I knew this will happen! Get up there the both of you! Now!" Paige harshly commanded. She failed to answer me directly again. Grabbing our hands firmly, Paige sprinted and pulled us to the rear door.

She immediately hurled two grappling hooks to the ledge and shouted for Jack and me to climb up as fast as we could. She did not explain anything, but it was obvious that Paige knew the beast was too dangerous for us to deal with. It might be too dangerous for both of us, but what about her?

As ordered, Jack and I desperately climbed the ropes attached to the hook. It was very taxing. Blisters were forming on my hands due to rope burn as I swayed back and forth to prevent myself from slipping off.

I looked down to see my feet five meters off the ground. Any careless fall meant broken legs. Jack held on to his rope with his left hand and his right reached into a pouch of his skin suit. He slipped out a disc-like piece of metallic device.

The device was The Exlecutor; the one which electrocutes and stuns the target.

"Hey, you ugly bastard! Jack has a little surprise for you!" He screamed down. Upon flicking the switch, he threw it at the creature below which was ready to prey on Paige.

He missed. I cursed.

The device struck the pavement beside the beast with a loud clang. The beast pawed Paige down and began its clawing rampage. The woman swung her fists into the beast's face to keep its bite away from her neck. Unfortunately, deep bloody gashes were already forming on her arms, staining her jacket.

She is going to die if this goes on! I thought.

I darted my head around to look for ways to help her. Panicky impeded my chain of thoughts.

Where is the brash and wise-cracking Koby whenever I need him? I scolded myself.

I noticed a pipe linking up the vertical wall right beside. Water was leaking out off it. The pipe was loose. An idea miraculously struck my mind. I increased my grip on the rope and swung back to gather momentum.

It was not enough.

I swung back and forth again for more momentum, but to no avail. My legs could not yet reach the pipe.

Then I swung backwards again. This time as I shifted my body weight to the front, I received a boost—an enormously hard kick to my butt that gave me the adequate momentum.

Jack kicked me really hard from the opposite rope. He deserved a thumbs-up.

Finally, my legs had the opportunity to contact the pipe for a split second. And within this crucial moment, I executed a front snap kick that landed hard on the loose water pipe. Water rushed out from it upon the screws coming loose.

"Paige! Get away from the pavement! Move to the grass patch!" I shouted at the top of my voice. This turned out to be not a covert mission anymore—we were all too loud.

The jet of water gushed down on the pavement. Paige rolled out safely into the grass patch. When the beast tried to do the same, it was too late. The downpour of water had covered the beast together with . . . the electrically charged Exlecutor.

There was a howl of pain. Volts of electrical waves mercilessly zapped across the beast. It did not stand a chance. When the charge of the device was depleted, the electrocution ceased. The beast laid on the pavement among a puddle of water, twitching and smoke diffusing from its skin.

Paige stood up from the grass patch, wiped her face and waved to us.

"Is it dead yet?" Jack called out.

"No!" Paige replied. We were disappointed. "But barely conscious, at least for quite some time. Come on! We've got work to do."

The three of us climbed up the rope onto the ledge.

After slipping on a pair of thin rubber gloves, Paige skillfully sliced open the window panel with a glasscutter she brought and placed the large piece of glass to the side of the ledge. We meticulously entered the study.

"If that beast wakes and climbs up. We've got this glass panel to drop on its head," I joked. The others ignored me. I changed the topic. "What in the world was it anyway?"

"Demons! Jack told you they exist!"

"You are about to find out," Paige pointed at the computer on the desk. "Now one of you should be able to hack into this right?"

"That would be Jack!" Jack volunteered. I was sure he was capable of doing it. Thus, I raised no objections.

Paige and I waited while Jack fiddled and meddled with the keyboard. I could tell that it was a complicated and intellectually demanding process, even if I was not the one doing it. The sheer numbers of algorithms, sequences and so on, were intimidating enough for me, whereas Jack seemed to handle it as if he was playing a video game.

About fifteen minutes later, Jack squealed in delight.

It was done.

On the computer screen, there was an abundance of files presented. Jack initiated a download sequence onto his hard disk. Once it was done, we took the same way out and left of the mansion.

The beast was still unconscious. For some reason, I pitied it.

In the evening, we went over to Jack's squalid house, since we had the necessary tools there. We opened the downloaded files on Jack's computer and true enough; there were receipts of foreign contract killers. There were also documents of illegal fund transactions—Darmor's embezzlement of church funds.

All these were perfect evidences against Darmor.

"Oh Damor. He'd still the old habit of keeping everything." Paige mocked and slowly shook her head.

I noticed something weird. The gashes and wounds on her face and arms were gone.

Before I could say anything about it, Jack caught our attention.

"Look at this file! What's Project Souler?" He clicked on the file and it opened.

There were schematics and blueprints in it—mostly chemical formulas and human anatomies. I did not understand what they were. But I did know what Souler was. It was the water from the fountain at church, the water that all Followers must religiously drink before the start of any congregations, although I had never drank it before.

Jack raised his brow and suggested.

"Let's ask BRAIN about . . ."

"Not necessary. I know what it is now," Paige frowned after browsing through those blueprints. "Darmor is using his chemicals on people who drank from the Souler"

I looked at the blueprints and Paige began explaining what it meant: Darmor had a colorless and odorless chemical agent in the Souler. The chemicals were able to make people passive; hence they would just follow anything they admire without second thought.

On a huge dosage, a person under its effect may eventually ignore everything around them. Darmor did not want this to happen as it was not his goal. And therefore, this explained why he reminded the Followers to drink in small quantities.

I began to see the big picture of everything—the chemical in the Souler was used on the Followers before congregations so that they would accept and agree with anything Pastor Darmor preached. Yet, it was impossible to make the poisoned people trust him if his sermons were preposterous. So he made all his sermons seemed orthodox, then he would slowly influence people to his unorthodox bidding. Those innocent Followers were not even aware of their own state.

"Whoa! A combination of mind-controlling drugs and personal charisma to brainwash people! That's just crazy." Jack exclaimed. Yes, Darmor was despicably crazy. And soon, justice would be served.

Jack clicked on the next file labeled as Project Soulex. I wondered what it would be since it sounded very much like *Souler*. This file contained a short journal and not blueprints or schematics, therefore I needed not Paige's explanation. It read:

Project Soulex is a huge success. I combined the Souler's essence with the Xtaphyll formula to create something totally different from the Souler's mind-clouding effects. It shall be called Soulex. I tested it on William and it worked! He mentally called upon hornets that fatally stung one of my test subjects. Project Soulex will be a part of my new era. It shall be used to punish those who are unworthy.

"Powers. Superhuman powers," Paige muttered. She was in a daze. "William has superhuman powers."

"Powers? Did Jack hear wrong? This Soulex thing bestows powers?" Jack stammered.

"Yes. I must have drunk the Soulex by accident back then before Darmor tried to kill me," She explained. "That's why I couldn't be harmed nor killed easily."

I was caught in disbelieve. That explained why she did not have a scratch from the beast's attack and also, the reason for her youthful appearance. Chronologically, she ought to be at least fifty years old! She had some sort of healing or immortality abilities. Although I felt spectacular by the existence of this, on the other hand, it was quite freakish.

"We call it accelerated cell regeneration, if you want the scientific term," Paige corrected me. "But I know I can be killed if my body parts are not intact, I think."

It appeared that all along Paige was aware of her superhuman abilities. But only till now was she aware that the Soulex was the cause of it.

"Then that beast that attacked us has to be part of Darmor's bizarre experiment!" I analyzed.

Paige agreed.

"If that's the case, then we must give the evidence to the cops and stop him fast before he comes for us! He might already know we sneaked into his house!" At the back of my head, I worried that Darmor might send that hornet man he mentioned in his journal, to claim our lives.

Who can predict what an intelligent but mad person is capable of doing? I thought.

"What are we waiting for? Jack will hand it to the police now." He withdrew the memory stick. Paige placed her hand over his.

"No. We hand it to Chief Inspector of Internal Security. Not the police." Paige requested.

"But Darmor isn't a terrorist. He is a criminal right?" Jack was puzzled.

I understood Paige's intention—the police would hand the evidence to their superior, Chief Inspector Jones Flight from the Criminal Investigation Bureau. He was an active member and one of the leaders in the Love of Crusano church. Or worse, he was a close friend to his religious mentor Pastor Darmor. No doubt he was susceptible to both the influence of the Souler and Darmor's charisma.

In addition, there was an incident when Darmor was under police investigation due to being suspected for embezzling the church funds. During the period of investigations, the Followers continued to trust his character and sparked off several crusades on the internet for the support of his innocence. After a few months, he was set free, much to the joy of these Followers. Although there were speculations that a conspiracy was in place since Jones Flight was in command of the investigation, the case was closed nonetheless.

Paige undeniably sensed an underhand deal. I did sense it too.

"He is poisoning a mass group of people. That is obviously terrorism hmm?" Paige clarified casually.

Jack shrugged in agreement.

Eropagnis Police Headquarter was located at the heart of Eropagnis city. The law enforcing force was indeed just as important to the city's survival as it had kept major crimes at bay for years. Many citizens of Eropagnis considered joining the force to be a great honor, but not for me.

At the main reception, a young receptionist warmly greeted us with a bright smile when we approached her. But her smile melted off when we requested to see Chief Inspector Carl Judgal from the Internal Security Department, which was also known as the ISD.

"I'm sorry. You cannot simply see anyone you like. You must make a report first." The receptionist apologized for rejecting our request.

We left the headquarters. We did not make any report. If we were to do so, no doubt the Criminal Investigation Bureau would be handling the case since the evidences we provided were meant to charge Darmor for contract killing and embezzlement. This meant that CI Jones Flight would be leading the investigation. Yes, we doubted his integrity since he was closely related to Darmor although we did not have proof yet. But neither anyone of us were willing to take that uncertain risk to allow history to repeat itself again.

"Darn! If only we could make it into an internal security issue!" Jack complained.

"We can." A brilliant but crazy idea flowed into my head. As if telepathically, Paige knew what I intended.

"Take a sample of the Souler out from the church's fountain as the evidence that it is poisoned." Paige said on my behalf.

"Aha! Genius! That should be Kob's task! He goes to church on weekends so it should be easy for him to . . ." Jack partially understood my idea. But, he failed to understand that I was not intending to do it during the weekends.

"No. We can't afford to wait for the congregation on the weekends to grab that sample," I elaborated on the idea. Darmor might already know that we broke into his house. Perhaps contract killers were on the way for us. "We do it now!"

Under the night sky, the chances of breaking into the church building would be higher. The element of darkness could bless us with stealth and most people who lived in church would be asleep.

"You've gotta be kidding! It is already 3am!" Jack was worried about the incoming dawn. He was right, we will all be dead if dawn breaks and everyone wakes.

"Then we've approximately a few hours to get it then. Let's get moving!" Paige clapped her hands to spur us.

We've broke into Darmor's mansion before, surely this should not be any more difficult right?

The Soulex Effect

We spent half an hour back at Jack's home to gear up for this new mission. Unlike the previous mission, this time we made a conscious effort to pack along quite a few Jack-invented defensive equipments; the familiar ones such as the Exlecutor and Nettingale, along with a few new ones.

The Rodlade. It was a steel baton, about forty centimeters in length, featuring a retractable rod. Jack termed it to be an ideal non-lethal melee weapon and he even showcased some of his "smooth" sword moves, very much to our amusement.

Then there was the *Distracto.* The device resembled a mini handheld recorder. It was indeed meant to record our voices but here was the catch; the Distracto can be thrown towards a distance and upon impact, it plays and amplifies the recorded voice. Thus, it was a gadget perfect for creating distractions and to get us out of a sticky situation.

Finally, it was the *Corrozer*, a tennis ball-sized sphere with a red button on it. Jack warned us never to use it unless it is the last resort; when the button is pressed, the sphere will break apart and it must be thrown immediately to unleash a fog of acidic smoke on multiple targets. That sounded the most morbid and brutal compared to the other gadgets.

It was clear to us that arming ourselves with these gizmos was a pre-requisite as we might face more of Darmor's horrific creations—ranging from mutated beasts to super powered maniacs—during the course of our mission.

"Give Jack your watch." Jack ordered and pointed to the treasured watch I was always wearing.

"What? Why?" I did not to want to. The Crusanity design on it was great, yet the watch was priceless because it was a birthday gift from Gwendoline. Even though she had Ronald as her boyfriend, I knew that Gwendoline would always be in my heart.

"Jack wants to integrate BRAIN into that watch, so that BRAIN is portable." Jack said.

"Integrate that artificial intelligence into my watch?" I questioned defensively.

"Yea! So if there are any subject questions you need to ask in the future, BRAIN can answer them when Jack cannot . . ." He replied melancholically. He might have thought that he will not make it out from this mission alive.

He did not intend to back away from this mission, hence he prepared for the worst.

Paige also understood what Jack was implying. It was definitely not a time to be pessimistic. She firmly rested an assuring hand on his shoulder. I rested mine on his other shoulder and started patting.

"Come on Jack. We are professional demon hunters! We are invincible against the forces of evil!" I consoled him. I could not believe those childish words came out from my mouth.

But it was worth it. Jack's facial expression brightened up and his confidence regained. He nevertheless took my watch and started to upload BRAIN into it.

"Thanks Kob. If that's the case, then BRAIN and Jack shall answer your questions in the future!" Jack beamed. Paige and I returned a smile.

Jack was truly a great friend. I could go back to college now and finally laugh at those students; laugh at some who treated him like a freak and laugh at their stupidity for taking a nice person like Jack for granted. But on second thought, I should not because I was once very much similar to them. And now I regretted it a lot.

As BRAIN came to life in my watch, I sincerely thanked Jack for this new gift. My watch was upgraded; there was a new micro digital screen above the clock, and the watch became a little heavier. Jack just told me to use it well.

Once we were done gearing up, we made our way to the Love of Crusano church. Many saw that place as a home but now to me, it was nothing more but an enemy's territory.

Unlike the colorfully lit Love of Crusano church during the weekends, the church building appeared dull and mundane. The church compound was plain darkness, at least for the next two hours—we were counting on it.

I naturally became the leader of this operation since I knew the church building relatively well. Paige was unsure about it even though she was a founding member of this church—too much renovation had been done during the course of her absence.

We used a small acetylene welder to melt the lock on the main double doors. The hinges creaked aloud when I slowly pushed open it. Paige hushed me and she went to the door hinges to spit on each of it, whereas Jack simply closed his own ears. I softly giggled at his ridiculous attempt to shut off the noise.

Paige's saliva worked well as a lubricant—I could barely hear a sound while opening the door. Then we surreptitiously strode pass the gloomy hallways. We were glad that no security cameras or alarms were in place. Maybe, the religious people believed that Crusano will divinely guard this sacred place from intruders. Yet I somewhat predicted Darmor should have some kind of security in place.

Maybe a beast creature similar to the one at his house may be guarding this area. I thought and stayed caution.

We increased our pace as we passed the living quarters. It was the only place with people inside, or probably even Darmor himself. The living quarters were offered to Followers who had no shelter; most of them were young orphans and some were adults who worked full-time at church. Darmor would not be so genuinely kind to help them, there must also be a hidden agenda behind this. Nevertheless, we hoped every single one of them was soundly asleep.

Suddenly, a shadowy figure emerged that the end of the corridor! We bolted around to take cover but the pathway was too narrow and straight. We were spotted.

"Huh? Who are you?" Judging from the squeaky voice, it was a child. We moved closer to take a better look and I was right. There was a little girl about seven years old, yawning and rubbing her eyes. She was one of the orphans who lived in the church.

"Hello! We are going to the washroom. We could not sleep either." Paige responded. It was pretty smart of her to pretend as though we were also Followers who lived in church!

"Okay. But Pastor Darmor says that males and females cannot go into the toilet together." The little girl yawned naively. Paige blushed. And the little girl walked off.

There was a sizzling sound and pale blue glow. An Exlecutor was in Jack's grasp, charged and ready. He focused his sight on that little girl.

"Wait! You can't be serious?" I tugged at him. He was clearly aiming to launch the electrocuting device at the child.

"She might be one of those demons in disguise. We need to knock her out." Jack recklessly claimed. But Paige and I refused to let him throw it. Even if the child might have been genetically altered by Darmor's chemicals, she was too innocent to be hurt and after all, she did us no harm.

Gwendoline was also one of the people who drank the Souler. Other than the chemical effects of passiveness, surely she is not a freak right?

Soon, Jack gave up the idea.

We entered the large hall of the church. Thin beams of the moonlight skewered through several clerestories on the ceiling and made the church interior more visible. The fountain was right ahead of us.

Paige drew out a little test tube from her pouch and stooped up the clear liquid which glimmered under the moonlight.

"Well, what have we got here?" A nefarious voice caused us to freeze on the spot. There were two middle-aged men strolling towards us from the corridor and right in front of them was the little girl we'd met earlier. She must have told on us.

"Jack told you so . . ." Jack whispered sarcastically.

The tall men were smartly dressed in collared shirts and velvet pants.

"William? Is that you?" Paige seemed to know one of the men.

"Yes Paige. It's been a while. As what Pastor has predicted, you're alive and youthful. Very beautiful." The man called William praised and clapped.

Jack and I were equally confused.

The other man roared like a beast. His muscles started to rapidly expand till the extent his shirt was ripped apart. The face was protruding out, his eyes growing bigger, teeth lengthening to fangs and a snout formed. It was the same type, or exactly the same leonine beast that attacked us at Darmor's mansion. I gulped.

"Run! Take the sample and get out of here!" Paige shouted desperately as she stuffed the Souler sample into my palm.

The beast howled and pounded towards us with incredibly unnatural speed. Paige speared forward and collided straight into it, after all, her self-healing factor prevented her from most harm. I just prayed the beast would not rip off her arm. I wondered if she could heal from that.

While Paige engaged an animalistic combat with that beast, William took a few steps forward, raised his hands and pushed against the air. There were huge yellowish lumps rising up from his arms. The hideous lumps were gliding across his veins and towards his fingertips. And when they reached the fingertips, the lumps squeezed their way out from his skin and revealed a hornet wasp in each of their place. There were countless of hornets together. Flapping their wings and humming a deafening buzz, the swarm came right at us.

"Oh shit!" Jack immediately whipped out the Corrozer, clicked on the red button and tossed it into the swarm of incoming hornets.

So much for him for saying that the Corrozer must be used only as a last resort.

Fumes of white acidic smoke exploded from the device among the killer swarm. Thankfully, the device worked fairly well as many hornets began to corrode and splattered all over the floor. But after a few seconds when the smoke cleared, there was still sizable amount of those little pests left.

Jack foolishly took out his Rodlade and swung it wildly at the hornets surrounding him. His efforts were futile—a swinging rod certainly could not fend off the swarm. I thought of a better idea by plunging into the fountain. I submerged into the cool water with a hard splash. Then, I realized it was the not the best idea when I accidently swallowed several gulps of the Souler. It tasted like plain water.

I choked and held my breath. The hornets were flying above the surface and beckoning me to be dumb enough to stick my head out. There was another huge splash. Someone dived into the fountain too. It was Jack; it looked like he gave up his idea of "rod versus wasps".

The fountain was very deep. I did not know that earlier until now. Our bodies were about ten meters apart from the bottom even after submerging into it. Then I saw Jack struggled under the water—he was running out of air. I looked up again and caught the unfortunate sight of the hornets still lingering above the surface. That hornet-spawning William obviously wanted us dead.

I had to do something or Jack might drown. In fact, we would both drown. I turned my head all around to look for something that could help, as I felt myself losing my breath.

A lever on the bottom caught my attention.

Whatever the lever was for, it was my only option. I arduously swam down and pulled it as hard as possible.

It clicked.

The lever seemed to generate a lot of bubbles which blocked my vision.

As if Jack and I can breathe in the air from the bubbles. I cursed in agony.

Wait, no. There was an opened manhole beside the lever. Water was actually draining from it!

The vacuum from the manhole clung onto Jack and me, forcefully sucking the both of us into it. Then, we both landed hard onto a concrete ground with water splashing onto us.

I sat up to look around. Jack laid down and heavily panted to recover some air. We were sucked into the underground tunnel of the church. I peered up and watched the manhole automatically sealing itself with a round metal cover.

The smell down here was horrible. I nearly puked.

"Yikes that was close. You got the sample?" Jack asked as slowly regained his breath. I nodded.

We walked along the filthy tunnels and more fumes of stench filled my lungs. The distance was long and we did not know where we were headed.

"Hey Kob, did you drink in any Souler water just now?" Jack asked casually.

"Yes, by accident," I told him honestly. He became more serious. And I asked, "You?"

"No, Jack didn't. Shucks! You drank it? Are you feeling alright?" Jack asked worriedly.

I hesitated for a moment. Yes, I felt good with nothing at all. The Souler's effect was supposed to make me more passive. But hey, how was I being passive?

After making a conscious effort to think about it, the Souler had already affected me! Because I was clearly aware of the Souler's negative effects beforehand and after I drank it down, I should be the one worrying about it first. Instead, I had just let it happen without even thinking of it!

"I am fine Jack. No worries man!" I knew I wasn't. But at least the effects were not excruciatingly detrimental.

We ran to the end of the tunnel. There was a vent in which we could crawl through. I whipped out my Rodlade and extended the steel rod, using it like a crowbar to remove the vent's metal cover. It was not easy. And Jack took over. His bigger muscles served us well—the cover came right off upon a few jerks. We entered the vent and crawled through the narrow tunnel.

The path led us into a room. It was unfamiliar to me. There were columns of shelves filled with test tubes, flasks and other weird chemicals.

"Whoa! Darmor actually has a secret lab down here in church!" Jack exclaimed. I shrugged.

We became rigid when a shadow started gaining ground in front of us. It was clearly the silhouette of the leonine beast! It was approaching. We turned and sprinted towards the same vent we came in from. Out of a sudden, a pair of firm arms pulled us under a nearby shelf.

"Huh? Paige? You're alright?" My voice sounded nonchalant. I ought to be much escalated to know that Paige was in one piece. I blamed the effects of the Souler I drank.

"Anyone of you drank the Souler back then?" She asked quietly.

"Jack didn't. But Koby proudly did." Jack replied.

"How much did you drink?" She asked again.

"Quite a lot I think." I admitted. "No big deal at all."

"Not good! With an over dosage, you may start to ignore everything around you after a few minutes." Paige became extremely panicky. I was not at all worried.

"You mean like an emo kid?" Jack teased.

"Not funny. I don't know a cure for this . . ." Paige continued and began thinking hard. "But another chemical can suppress it."

"Wait. Jack remembers. That Xtaphyll thing right?" Jack recalled. I remembered this term too. The combination of the Souler and Xtaphyll would result in a chemical compound called Soulex. And Souler's active effect will be nullified, but the Soulex will genetically alter the host's deoxyribonucleic acid (DNA) structure. But the Soulex's effect differed between every individual; some gained superhuman abilities such as fast healing or hornet summoning, whereas the other became a hideous leonine beast.

But why bother? I thought.

The leonine beast moved closer to us. I could hear its heavy breath, saliva from its mouth leaking onto the flooring.

"Now where are the little piggies?" William taunted. He was with the leonine beast. But it did not matter to me. The situation would be equally bad even if he was not there, I think. The both of them were only two meters away from us. It would be a matter of time for us to be detected.

Jack reached to his pack and took out an Exlecutor and two Distracto devices. Along with my Rodlade, they were all the defensive tools left.

The Exlecutor was excluded from use—it became malfunctioned after Jack submerged into the water earlier. And on the other hand, the Rodlade might be able to fight against the leonine beast, but absolutely not William's hornets. We had to depend on the two Distracto devices.

Jack whispered into the Distracto's voice recorder and hurled it at the doorway. When Paige asked Jack what he had recorded, the answer came from a booming amplified voice at the doorway.

"I am here you mutated freaks!"

The distraction caught the attention of the leonine beast. We could hear its large feet racing towards the source of Jack's voice and away from our position. Paige and Jack gave a sigh of relief. I just grinned.

Unfortunately, William did not fall for the trick. Our muscles tensed. He must have sensed that the voice was false. This was indeed an excellent example of the old adage. *A man is always smarter than a beast.*

Jack prepared the remaining Distracto. And casually dropped it right onto the floor below us, the device emitted the same booming voice. It was deafening at close range.

"I am here you mutated freaks!"

I froze in fear despite being under the Souler's effect. Jack just sounded the alarm right in front of us! We were sure to be detected by William.

"You careless fool! What have you done?" Paige murmured angrily and elbowed Jack in the hips.

Jack said nothing. From the view of William's shadow projected onto the floor, William was actually walking away from us!

"Reverse psychology. That hornet wasp freak hears my voice projected from right here, and he will think it is just another ruse." Jack winked cheekily

"Good quick-wittedness! Now let's find the Xtaphyll among these shelves. Koby needs it." Paige said urgently.

We crawled out from under the shelves and made sure the coast was clear.

"You know that William guy?" Jack randomly asked.

"Yes, he was Darmor's best friend and his best man during our wedding," Paige answered. "Now shut up and start searching."

Then, Paige and Jack began to search through the shelves for the Xtaphyll. I did nothing but stood there and watched.

It doesn't matter to me. I am feeling good and alright. I don't need any help. I thought.

"There!" Paige drew out a syringe from a shelf and came at me, fully ready to inject the chemical into my body.

"The effects will be unknown but trust me; at least you will have control of yourself." She assured me. I shrugged nonchalantly.

Before the syringe's needle penetrated my skin, a blurred shadowy motion knocked Paige off the ground and sent her crashing into the shelves. I found myself staring into the glowing green slit eyes of the leonine beast. Jack tackled the beast from the side but he was yanked away.

William came into the lab. Hornets were flocking around him.

"Good trick. We'd both fell for it. Too bad there is only one doorway for this room and you could not have left without us noticing." William mocked. "And true enough, we've found you little scums still in here."

The hornets were coming right at me. I submitted to fate. As I stood there motionless, my eyes glazed over.

No! Something within me was telling me to get moving. I looked over to Paige and Jack. The leonine beast had both of their necks in its punishing grip. Their faces were turning purple and they were struggling to breathe. They were badly choking.

Paige should be okay eventually since she has powers. What about Jack? Well, he should be okay too since he is very smart right? Besides, a great god Crusano will watch over and protect them them. There is nothing to worry about. I thought.

No! What was I even thinking? My hands held tightly onto my head and I shook it violently. I was beginning to feel the horrible effects of the Souler. In my head, I heard Darmor's voice and felt myself sitting down at a congregation.

"Once we accept Crusano to be our god and give up everything to him, everything in our mortal lives will be prosperous!" He said, triggering a wave of applause from the Followers. It was from one of his sermons I remembered.

I screamed in pain as I tried to shake my mind out of this. Then, another part of his sermon came to my mind.

"But to get Crusano's blessing, we must always trust our pastor and leaders. To listen and honor them in everything!" And everyone clapped.

"Crusano is the only true god . . ." I found myself subconsciously mouthing these words.

A stinging pain surged up my arm and brought me back to my senses. I swept away a hornet from my foreman, but there was a large sting embedded into my flesh. More hornets were only a meters away from me. I was in a daze. Paige and Jack were still within the grip of the beast.

They're in trouble . . . I told myself.

No! They're in serious trouble! I must help! I slapped myself hard in the face.

With quick reflexes, I bent downwards, picked up the syringe filled with Xtaphyll and did an evasive roll away from the hornets. I gave myself a jab in the arm.

"Even if I am going to become a monster, so be it!" I yelled and compressed the Xtaphyll agent into my bloodstream.

I waited for its effects. Nothing.

The hornets were onto me. They harassed me by their pesky stings. One or two was considered pesky. But three or more would be fatal. I aggressively shrugged them off, hoping to unleash whatever Soulex power that I was supposed to have.

I wanted the power to spurt fire—to burn these hornets and set that leonine beast on fire to save my friends. I wanted the power to teleport—to poof out of here along with my friends. Or perhaps I wanted the power to . . . get these hornets to stop attacking me.

I collapsed onto the ground and covered my face with my arms. The hornets were merciless. My limbs were swelling up from their stings.

Stop! Please stop this right now! I begged.

They stopped. I opened my arms and looked at the hornets. They were just hovering around me without any further assaults.

"Don't just stay there! My children! Finish him!" William commanded the hornets.

The hornets once again moved towards me.

Stop! I held up my arms again to shield my face.

The hornets ceased. I was surprised.

Despite having no injury, Paige was too weak to fight back against the leonine beast. Jack had reached the maximum amount of punishment he could endure. He was barely conscious with his head and arms bleeding profusely.

"Kob . . . run . . ." I could hear his weakening voice murmuring.

Jack. He was worrying for me even though he was in grave danger. And if I'd just considered my own safety, I would be inhumane.

How I wished those hornets were stinging on that leonine beast instead of me. I wanted revenge on that beast for what it had done on Paige, and done worst on Jack. I was filled with rage. I swore I would make it suffer the same way.

"Why get satisfied by stinging a little me? There is a bigger and juicier target up ahead." I unknowingly chanted. My head was feeling very heavy. My brain felt like exploding.

The hornets charged towards the leonine beast.

PERSONALITY MAGNIFIER

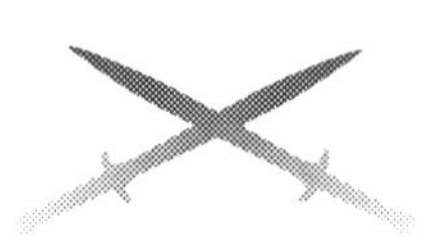

THE KILLER SWARM engulfed the beast, stinging it even more viciously than ever. The beast howled in pain as I watched it get tortured by those little bugs. And within seconds, the leonine beast was dead. Its body was very much more hideous; huge stings all over its hide with yellow pus squirting out from the cysts.

What just happened? I have powers to control the hornets? Then that makes two hornet-controlling freaks!

"Good job! Let's see how you do this." Hornet-controlling freak number one William challenged me. He snapped. The swarm came back towards me, along with another swarm he had just spawned from his arms.

I will be dead within seconds under the attack of so many of them. So I attempted to use my abilities to counteract it.

"Err . . . why get satisfied by stinging a little me? There is a bigger and juicier target up ahead!" I deliberately repeated the chant from earlier. It did work back then, but not now. The swarm was once again onto me.

I did not bother to communicate with those wasps anymore. I navigated the room and spotted a large window directly behind William. An idea struck my mind; I could dive straight through the swarm towards William and crash him through the window. It might be fatal and although I have not murdered anyone in my life, it was a situation between life and death.

I visualized myself pushing William off the window—the glass shattering, his body flying through the air and slamming down onto the ground below. It felt good.

Before I took a first step forward to initiate my strategy, William spontaneously jumped backwards and crashed out of the window.

"What?" He screamed hysterically as he flew out and disappeared, followed by a loud bone-cracking thud.

I was stunned. He did exactly what I had planned. And I did not even lay a finger on him!

The hornets around me dispersed. Some of them flew out of the broken window. I was finally safe.

I went back to Paige and Jack who were sprawling on the floor among the broken shelves and glass fragments.

"I'm fine. Just feeling weak and exhausted," Paige coughed. "But I am not sure about him though."

Jack's eyes were closed. He was motionless. Blood was dripping down his body. I was so afraid he was dead.

"Jack! Jack!" I called out. He should be okay, he *must* be okay. *Please.*

"Kob? Paige? You're alive? Or are we all dead?" Jack slowly opened his eyes and sat upright. He used his sleeve to wipe off the blood on his face. Paige and I hugged him as tears of joy flowed down our cheeks.

"Ouch! Thanks guys. Now we had better get out of here. The sky is getting brighter." He smiled faintly.

"Yes, we have to leave, but how?" Paige did not know how she even got here in the first place. No doubt, the church building was very large and its architecture was complex.

I was unfamiliar to which part of the church this secret lab was located. But the artificial intelligence programmed into my watch should know. After all, it was called the Brilliant Robotic Artificially Intelligent Navigator. It ought to be able to navigate our way out of here.

"BRAIN. From our location, what's the best way out?" I raised the watch to my mouth and asked.

"Your question involves the most updated architecture of the Love of Crusano church from Eropagnis city. The nearest exit will be . . ." BRAIN's monotonous voice guided us the way back to the vent in which Jack and I used. The vent led three of us to the same smelly underground tunnel. From there, BRAIN directed us to a second vent that was connected to the streets outside through a manhole. Dawn came and we returned to Jack's house.

After a good shower and applying some ointment to smooth the swells on my arms, I borrowed Jack's home phone to call Aunt Joan. My mobile phone was damaged during the night raid. From her tone, she clearly missed me as much as I dearly missed her. But of course, I told her that I will be coming back from my friend's place after we finished our school project.

Jack twisted the screwdriver into place as he fixed his malfunctioned gadgets. At certain intervals, he would tighten the bandages wrapped around his shoulder and head. Paige was sorting out the evidences that we were going to present to the Internal Security Department. She was the only one who did not need any bandages or medicine.

This is finally coming to an end. I thought. Gwendoline, Pierre, Ronald and all the other Followers who were deceived by Pastor Darmor for so long, will finally see the light of truth. Darmor's selfish and cruel plans would soon come to an end.

"So, what powers did you acquire from the Soulex?" Jack asked excitedly. I did not reply him. I was not sure myself.

Shall I call it the power of hornet-controlling and sending—people—right off—the—window?

"I saw what happened. I believe that you can mentally bend the will of others to your bidding," Paige clarified. "Let's try it out."

We stood in formation as instructed by Paige—I stood alone at an end of the room while she and Jack stood at the other end, far apart from me. Then, she used a piece of cloth to tightly wrap around my mouth to prevent me from speaking. I wondered what she planned to test.

"We'll do this fast as we must deliver the evidence soon," She said. "Now Jack, I want you to close your eyes and think of nothing. Keep it that way until I say so."

Jack complied. He was giggling ebulliently like a child waiting to receive a Christmas present.

"Think of nothing Jack!" Paige reminded him, shutting up his giggles. "Koby, watch this!"

She took a screwdriver and erected it on the floor in front of her. The sharp point of it was facing upwards. Out of a sudden, she leaned forward and dropped straight down towards the screwdriver!

I was shocked. I desperately wanted to grab her or the screwdriver could penetrate into her heart! But I was out of range.

Wait, the screwdriver alone cannot harm Paige right? Her powers will negate the fatal blow and . . . whatever, I could not bear the gory sight.

I shouted to Jack who was standing right next to her, hoping he would open his eyes and to grab Paige instead. Unfortunately, only an inaudible muffled noise sounded from my covered mouth.

But before Paige landed on the sharp point, Jack's hands reached out to grab her, thus preventing the fall. His hands were on her breasts.

"What? What's this? Pretty squishy." Jack asked curiously with his eyes still closed. He unknowingly squeezed Paige's breasts a couple of times. Paige's face turned bright red. I pulled out the piece of cloth around my mouth and burst into laughter.

Now I understood what she meant by mentally bending people's will—I utilized my mind to control Jack's thoughts and actions even if he was unaware of it! That explained how I ordered the hornets to sting that beast creature and how I caused William to jump out off the window on his own.

Cool! My powers work on both humans and animals alike! I was astounded

"Ahem. Jack. Kindly open your eyes and see how much psychological damage you've done to a girl." Paige joked embarrassingly.

Jack's eyes slightly opened, and then his eyes opened really wide. He gasped and immediately withdrawn his hands from Paige's breast.

"Feels good huh?" I teased him. His face turned red and he said nothing.

"Okay enough jokes. Now Koby remember, your powers can only work when the target isn't putting up a mental resistance against it," She warned me. She seemed to know a lot of things about this. "In other words, don't overly rely on it."

I nodded. I was excited about my new found powers. The much fun I could have with it. I imagined myself making a fool out of everyone I disliked by manipulating them to do stupid antics. The feeling of having abilities above the average man was splendid.

I would be more superior to the others.

The next few days of my life were heavenly. After Paige submitted the evidence to the Internal Security Department, Pastor Darmor became a fugitive. He was on the run but nowhere to be found.

Church activities were suspended and all the Followers were required to attend a medical checkup at the Eropagnis General Hospital. Each took a dosage of antidote to neutralize the Souler chemical agent in their bodies. It was not entirely a permanent cure for sure but it worked well to rid the effects.

Followers at college still formed Crusanity meetings to pray together. There was no harm to it, yet the college authorities banned them from this activity. Pastor Darmor's bad reputation had implicated the religion itself. Now everyone thought that Crusanity was nothing more than an unorthodox cult. This belief also led to a series of mobs initiated by street protestors, who were mostly the family members of the Followers. Some Followers who were angered by Darmor's plot also joined the mob. Fortunately, there was no riot. Some might just call it a peaceful protest.

There was only a news report of a man stung to death by hornets in the church premises. On the news footage, he looked human and no longer the leonine beast. Perhaps, he evolved back into his original form upon death. As for William, he was neither mentioned nor found at all. Thus, he might be still alive and somewhere out there.

Darmor somehow got rid of all his chemicals at the church hidden lab; the Souler, Xtaphyll and everything that linked to his research. It might be considered both good and bad news; bad news being scientists were not able to do a research on those dangerous stuff and on the other hand, good news being no one could get their hands on it.

When I went back to college, I could hear students joking about Jack and me being a couple again. Due to both of our absence for the previous days, they joked that we were attempting to elope but failed.

Wait till I use my powers to make a joke out of all you.

A physics test was round the corner, but I did not study for it as I was busy busting Darmor's crime for the last few days. At first I wanted to seek academic help from Jack, yet I was too lazy to do so since I wanted to spend my extra time to rest from our adventure. And before I even realized it, the test had started.

My hands became sweaty and I twirled my pen to keep calm. The questions were rather challenging, at least for someone who did not study for it. But I did not want to fail this test and give myself a poor reputation in this prestigious college. I breathed faster as I watched the time helplessly flew by.

I turned my head to see a classmate whose name was Peter, scribbling confidently on his script beside me. He would be a perfect candidate for my source of answer.

I took in a deep breath and mentally told him to go to sleep. A slight headache was forming and I stayed focus. As his eyelids became heavy, Peter slumped onto the table. One of the invigilators was strolling towards my direction. I used the same technique on him; increasing his will for him walk somewhere else. The attempt was successful and I was proud of myself.

I stealthily moved to Peter's desk, glanced at his answer script and memorized almost everything off it. The other students were too busy writing their scripts to notice me. Then, I went back to my desk and photocopied Peter's answers on my script. And within seconds, I had completed my whole test paper.

According to the clock at the front of the class, there was still five minutes left. I wanted to fruitfully kill this time. I glanced around the examination hall. And I saw several students who were familiar; they were the ones who loved to mock and pass insulting comments about Jack and me.

It is time for them to learn their lesson. I thought.

There were about five of these students I identified. Using my powers, I made two of them fell asleep so that their script could not be completed. I made another two scribbled nonsense on their papers then brought them to sleep so that they would be submitting a script full of nonsensical markings.

And the last one was called Nelson, he was probably the worst among all. The rich boy insulted almost anyone who did not appeal to his eyes. I really wanted to try something more amusing—I shall make him jump on the table and let him scream and dance like a monkey.

Nelson did exactly what I had intended. Everyone was stunned for a moment, and then all the students laughed their hearts out while the invigilators tried to restrain him. I grinned.

That clown was escorted out of the examination hall, giving an extremely bewildered look when my effects on him died out. He was officially barred from the test.

As the timer sounded, I simply arranged my answer scripts properly and handed it over to the invigilator who came to collect it. And I looked at Peter and I saw the invigilator knocking on his desk to wake him up.

On the way out of the examination hall, Jack hopped to me and asked.

"How was the paper?"

"It was fine. Good." I replied.

"Wow! You saw what happened just now? That lunatic just got possessed by some kind of monkey. Scary but funny!" Jack commented.

"Well perhaps he got a little too stress." I gave him my false stand. In fact, I knew I was responsible for that commotion. But it did not matter to me since what was done was already done.

And besides, there is no harm putting up a little entertainment to ease the stressful examination environment. I thought.

The test period was the last session in school. The streets were packed when I was on my way home. It was the peak hour. Members of the labor force and school students were rushing home from work after a laborious day. I wanted some rest too—using my powers can be quite mentally taxing,

As I crossed the train platform, I saw Ronald and Gwendoline together again. Their hands were held tight and they were nudging each other intimately. I thought that after the suspension of the church, they were no longer together, since Ronald only met Gwendoline at church. I was dead wrong.

The feelings of jealously overwhelmed me again.

I liked Gwendoline so much ever since middle school and just because I was sceptical to Love of Crusano church's teachings, she detests me?

I was aware that I was being over sensitive and paranoid since Gwendoline had never said she detests me. Besides, with Pastor Darmor's true intentions exposed, she ought to be apologizing to me. All in all, I knew there was not a need to indulge in self-pity.

I have powers you know. I reminded myself.

From a distance, I channelled my energy towards my brain. I wanted to humiliate Ronald in front of Gwendoline to show that I was the better man.

My mind-bending powers succeeded again. Ronald's left hand brushed against another female passenger's bottom. The molested victim gave him a tight slap across his face and stormed away. A second slap hit his face and this time, much to my pleasure, it was from Gwendoline.

"Gwen! No, I didn't . . ." Ronald explained in vain and Gwendoline walked off in rage. All the passengers on the train platform gave him an unfriendly look. I loved it.

For the rest of the evening, I kept rhapsodizing on Ronald's expression when the ladies slapped him. It was priceless. So what if he was our church leader. So what if he was better looking and more charming than I was. I would not give in anything to him, especially a girl I like, ever.

This power is indeed making my life more worthy and interesting. I thought. *And I love it.*

RESCUE

FROM MY BEDROOM, I gave Gwendoline a call to comfort her on what had happened today. I just wanted her to know that I will be there for her no matter what. When she picked up, I could hardly recognize her voice as she was sobbing too loudly. I had never in my life heard her like this, until now.

"I saw what happened today as I took the train home too. I am sorry." I feigned innocence.

"Ronald is a nice guy! I don't think he did it on purpose. I was just so embarrassed today when that lady hit him. That's why I hit him too!" Gwendoline sobbed.

I felt sorry for her. That joke was meant to be played on Ronald yet, I unintentionally hurt Gwendoline in the process. I regretted it.

"It is okay. I will always be here for you. I've always been here for you." I strongly hinted my affections for her. Perhaps, this was the first time I went that far. No doubt my new found powers also gave me some confidence.

"Thanks Kob. You're a great friend. But I don't think I want to get into a relationship for now." Gwendoline replied. I was slightly disappointed but at least, the other guys at college would not stand a chance too.

Ever since the start, although I liked her a lot, I never had the intention for her to be my girlfriend. I just wanted her company. And of course, I constantly get a little envy whenever she hung out with other people, especially guys.

Since she was a faithful believer of Crusano, I used the name of this god to encourage her.

"Don't worry. You're a great girl. Crusano will give you the best husband in the future. Everything will be okay," I consoled her. "Remember what you once told me?'

She paused.

"*Faith is being sure of the unseen and believing in what you do not yet see.*" I preached.

"Yes. I am always faithful to Crusano. But ever since Pastor Darmor's plight, I had realized one thing in life Koby." She regained her voice. "*But if our faith is not rewarded, it will be nothing but the greatest deception of life.*"

I knew what she meant—Gwendoline had always been faithful to church, to Crusano, to our leader Ronald and Pastor Darmor. But Darmor's diabolical acts had gravely disappointedly her. And now Ronald—indirectly, it was me.

"I am sorry Gwendoline." I sincerely felt apologetic. I should not have destroyed the relationship between the both of them. Gwendoline indeed looked up a lot to Ronald. I really did not know what came over me when I did that trick to Ronald. Was it pure jealously? Or was it selfishness?

"Don't apologize, Kob. It's not your fault." She said, and her sobbing stopped. I begged to differ.

Her ruined relationship with Ronald was my fault

"Well maybe you can give Ronald a call and talk things out?" I suggested reluctantly. I knew it was dumb of me to give Ronald a second chance to be together with Gwendoline, but it was the right thing for me to do, for all the damage I had caused.

"Yes. I guess you are right. I shouldn't hurt someone I love just because of a silly misunderstanding," She sounded much better and I felt happy. "Good night Koby. Thank you so much."

She hung up the phone. I was filled with a sudden raw peace unlike anything I had felt before. I dropped back on the bed and mouthed a silent blessing for Ronald and Gwendoline.

If I really love her, her happiness will be just as important as mine. I thought.

The weekends approached. But there was not any church congregation to attend, perhaps until someone is willing to take over Pastor Darmor's leadership. But in the light of the anti-Crusanity protesters roaming around the streets, no one was bold enough to take up this responsibility.

I somehow felt that there was too much spare time to kill, hence after doing my homework, I went to Chopper's Cafe to grab a bite.

"Welcome!" I was greeted a familiar voice as I gently slide opened the door and entered the cafe.

"Paige! You're the owner of this cafe?" I exclaimed upon seeing my friend.

"Yes. It has always been my bread and butter," Paige's eyes gleamed. She was dressed in a brown apron with the words *Chopper's Cafe* printed on it. "Today's meal is on the house!"

I sat down at one of the round tables and made an order of bolognaise with minced meat and mozzarella cheese. It was Gwendoline's favourite. I just want to "eat" away the past and forget about her.

While waiting for the food to be prepared, I stood up and went to the toilet.

"Don't forget to see the mirror for bloodied words." Paige told me teasingly. I remembered the words which was scribbled in blood on the mirror when I came here the previous time. Paige was indeed the one who did it to frighten me as the demon.

"So you used your own blood to write?" I challenged her light-heartedly.

"Nah! It was a dead pig's blood you fool!" She then went into the kitchen.

The toilet that day was very clean. An aromatic perfume diffused in the air. I loved it. And when I was done taking a leak, I went back to my table.

Paige took a sit beside me and placed my plate of food with a cup of water on the table. She then slipped off her apron.

"How's business?" I asked.

"Good as usual. Is it very stressful studying in the National College of Eropagnis?" She replied and asked casually.

"Not that bad," I honestly told her. "Why?"

"According to the newspaper today, a student called Nelson committed suicide." Paige said. "Some of the students said that he went berserk during a recent test. Quite a pitiful boy."

I froze rigid. Then, I requested Paige to bring me the newspaper. She took them from behind the cash register and handed it over to me. I read it in disbelieve.

Nelson's parents had very high expectations on him. After the incident when he behaved like a monkey and was barred from the physics test, his parents badly chided him. No matter how he tried to explain himself, his parents would not listen. They grounded him and forced him to break off with his girlfriend. I knew he loved his girlfriend very much since she was the only person who he did not insult. And under such immerse pressure, Nelson jumped off his apartment block.

"What . . . what have I done?" Such guilt was horrible. *I have accidently took an innocent life just for my own amusement, leaving his loved ones to grieve.*

"Koby, what are you saying?" Paige snapped her fingers at me.

"Nothing," I lied and turned my eyes away.

The cafe bell rang as the door sprang opened.

"Welcome!" Paige spun back and greeted her customer.

It was Ronald. He was dressed in an odd manner, with a flak jacket, track pants and military boots.

"Koby! I need your help. Gwen's in trouble." Ronald called out to me.

I dared not draw any conclusion from this, I just asked him to take a seat first to hear him out.

"Look, Gwen was abducted. I investigated her phone and found your number on the very same night of her abduction," Ronald spoke, panting. "What did she say to you?"

No. That's impossible. I just could not believe that!

"Nothing much, our conversation was just the normal stuff." I replied. I wondered what he meant by he investigated her phone. Was he trying to be his own policeman?

"We have to call the cops!" I blurted out panicky.

Gwendoline is very important to me. I can't afford to lose her. I swore.

"The police can't do much but I can!" Ronald claimed confidently.

"What do you mean you can?" I argued.

"You're Ronald, right?" Paige interrupted. She picked my fork from table and stabbed it into her own hand without hesitation.

Ronald's jaw dropped. Blood was oozing out from her hand. Then, she picked up a table cloth and wiped the blood away.

There was no sign of any wounds.

Ronald smiled.

"I see. Then you must be Paige Chopper, the first lady who took in Soulex and became almost invincible." Ronald praised her. I did not know they knew each other!

"Alright, I sagaciously infer that Koby and you are aware of Pastor Darmor's plot hmm?" Ronald continued. Paige nodded.

Before I could voice out my confusion, Paige shook hands with Ronald and she turned to me.

"His real name is Ross. He is a member of the Auzora organisation which deals with exceptionally dangerous people like Darmor." Paige introduced. She was indeed a woman who knew a lot of things

"Auzora?" I did not know what that meant.

"Auzora is a derivation from the Japanese word *blue sky*," Ronald, who was now called Ross, explained. "Our organization's goal is to make these dark days bright and blue again."

"You mean dark days because of the existence of people like Darmor? You mean he abducted Gwendoline?" I inferred. With my heart pounding nervously, I was clear that Darmor was a very dangerous man—I could tell from his two atrocious minions; Willliam and the leonine beast. And now, the fact that Gwendoline was within his clutches, scared me.

"Yes. He abducted her." Ross said.

"But he is on the run! Why did he return to kidnap her?" I questioned nervously. *Why must it be her?*

"Gwendoline is one of his best creations. She is an artificial human replicated from Darmor's own DNA." Ross continued explaining. "But he lost her when our organization raided his laboratory years ago. Gwen was later adopted by a pair of loving couples."

He took a sip from my cup water, and explained further.

"I made myself a leader of the church so that I could investigate on him. And I went steady with Gwendoline so that . . ."

"So that you can make use of her to help you bring Darmor to justice!" I shouted in anger. I was infuriated because Gwendoline truly loved Ross, yet he was just treating her like a tool for his mission.

"Yes. But you guys cracked the case faster than I," Ross sarcastically applauded. "But in actual fact, I need to stay close to Gwen because I have to keep an eye and make sure Darmor is not aware than she was the baby he created.

"Why?" Paige asked.

"Let's just say she is the perfect weapon he made for himself." Ross said and squinted.

Weapon? It sounded bad enough to me already to learn that Gwen is an artificial human made from maybe a test tube. And now, she is a weapon?

"What kind of weapon?" I was worried.

"It doesn't matter. If things do not work out well, we take Gwen down too," Ross replied. "I doubt he has left Eropagnis city yet. No sign of his trace at any immigration checkpoints".

I hated the sound of that—Darmor's still here. But at least, there was still a chance to save Gwendoline.

"Now, we do not know where she is held captive right?" Paige asked.

"That's why I am here to ask Koby . . ." He stated the intention of his visit again.

"I do!" I said. "Darmor's mansion. No one knows he has that mansion."

"Perfect!" Paige cheered.

"Okay, lead me there. Then you can take your leave." Ross told me harshly.

"No! I am helping you." I objected. I made a promise to Gwendoline that I will always be there for her. And other then that, I ought to redeem myself for all the sins I had done, especially the way I caused Nelson's suicide. It was not intentional of course, but it was undeniably my fault. And also, the cheating and sabotaging during the test added more fire to my guilt. I could not live with myself like that.

"You might get yourself killed!" Ross argued. He was right. I might not be as lucky as my previous encounter with super powered hostiles. But that did not change my mind.

"Don't worry. Koby has the Soulex encrypted onto his DNA. He can help. That goes the same for me." Paige stood up for me.

Ross shook his head but he eventually agreed reluctantly.

Before we should contact the Internal Security Department to send their units to arrest Darmor, we ought to confirm whether or not Darmor was really holding Gwendoline captive in his mansion. Anyway, Ross would not allow us to contact any mainstream department as he had absolute confidence that his Auzora organization can handle the situation. Surely, I thought it might be a fool's hope.

We made no preparation for this task as every second wasted might increase the likelihood of Gwendoline's full evolution, according to Ross, whatever that actually meant.

I suggested to them for Jack to assist us in this mission but Ross and Paige cohesively refused; the former preferred one less person to join this mission while the latter was concerned about Jack's recovery. Therefore, I dropped the idea.

Darmor's mansion still looked the same like before, but this time as we got closer, we saw that his security system had been greatly enhanced; there were three leonine beasts guarding the front yard. They were very hungry for human flesh. These beasts looked slightly different from the one we encountered before—the ones now walked on all four limbs whereas the previous walked on only two.

"No. No. My poor Nicole, Ling and Karn., what have that monster done to you?" Paige cried in melancholy.

Now, I could recognize the identities of these beasts. They were the Rottweilers which Paige loved dearly ever since they were little puppies. I felt sorry for them to undergo this ordeal.

"Now bend their wills! Take away their desire to attack any of us." Ross ordered me rudely. I was irritated but complied nonetheless.

My face and brain was feeling hot as I directly my powers onto all three of the creatures. As we climbed over the main gates and sneaked past them, the three creatures just stared at us.

Panic gripped my spine when Paige ambled towards the creatures.

"Paige. Don't do that. I am not sure how long I can hold." I cautioned her and tried very hard staying focused.

She ignored me.

"They will kill her!" I attempted to rush forward and pull her back, but Ross held me back instead.

"She will be fine if you just stay focus!" Ross appeared to be more confident in my power than I was. I made no further attempts to move.

Bending down beside those monstrous beasts, Paige began patting their heads and stroking their backs. Tears flooded her eyes and she was sniffing to hold it back.

Then, she raised a hand as if she was giving a signal.

Out of a sudden, three crossbow bolts each found their mark on every beast's head, claiming their lives. I looked beside me and Ross was there holding a semi-automatic crossbow pistol in a firing position. Then, he slowly lowered his weapon and reloaded it.

"Thank you, Ross. For helping me end their suffering." Paige swept off her last drop of tear and walked back to us.

"They do not deserve such fate, even if they are animals." Ross comforted her.

We moved towards the main door solemnly.

Courage for Beloved

Ross had explosives with him. I initially thought that this might be another stealth mission but I was wrong. He planted a detonation pack on the main door and activated it, thus sending the huge wooden door shattering into pieces.

He was the first one to rush in the mansion with a military-styled manner. It looked cool. The arm which held his crossbow crossed on top of the other arm, which was bending perpendicularly and firmly locked in place. It was a tactical aiming position for steady accuracy. I've seen it on television.

Ross is out for blood.

We entered main hall of the mansion. The interior was breathtaking—an image of a grand palace with the expensive sofas, curtains, lamps, ornaments and there were two large spiral stairs curling up to the second floor. Living in there was everyone's dream.

Something snapped me out from reverie. There was a movement on the ceiling, behind a chandelier. Ross and Paige were scouting around but they had failed to notice it. Then, the thing scooped down on us with a frightening shriek.

It was clad in hooded black robes with pale white face, malevolent yellow eyes, fangs and hooked claws. Most terrifyingly, it had wings—feathered and black—which allowed flight.

It struck me first in the chest with its strong talons. I was painfully tossed and collided onto the wall, forcing me to vomit blood out.

Paige gripped aggressively onto its legs to hold it down while Ross took an aim. He was probably the best marksman I've ever seen. Despite the rapidly moving target, his aim was true and several of his crossbow bolts penetrated the winged creature's neck.

But to our horror, the creature simple plugged off the bolts and its gaping wounds recovered, similar to what Paige could do.

I regained my composure and concentrated hard to manipulate its will to my bidding. The creature jerked for a second. It shrugged off Paige like a ragdoll and opened its mouth wide at me.

Before I reacted, a blast of sonic shriek slammed into me. I was critically stunned and felt ill. Soon, more vomit came out from my throat. The feeling was torturous.

Ross was the best fighter among us. He leaped onto the creature's back and gave it a punishing headlock. The winged creature was struggling to breathe as it swung its claws in a futile attempt to hit Ross off it. Then, it dropped onto the ground, shrieking ferociously with Ross pinning it down.

"Most impressive, Ronald. I didn't know you are a spy from Auzora. And to think I trusted you." An old and deep voice came from a distance with sounds of applause. It was Darmor. To my eyes, he had became a complete contrast of what he was as a pastor in church; he was no longer the charismatic and respectable man everyone knew but rather, he became a crazy, ambitious and cruel statue of evil.

Darmor was in some sort of armor which protected his entire body except the head; shiny white and blue plate metals. One of his hands held on a long, sharp and elegant cyan sword. He resembled the image of Crusano as described in the doctrines.

"Where's Gwen?" Ross shouted in rage as he continued struggling to keep the winged creature pinned.

"How unobservant are you? You are holding on to her, aren't you?" Darmor hinted.

Ross jaw dropped. So did mine.

No! No! No! What has he turned Gwendoline into?!

The winged creature took advantage of this distraction and knocked Ross off and sent him sprawling onto the ground. He hurriedly picked up his crossbow pistol and took aim again. But he did not fire.

The creature, no, Gwendoline flew beside Darmor and landed onto the railing of the staircase. I could see the facial features clearly now. It was indeed the beautiful and kind Gwendoline who I loved so much. Now, she was emotionless and totally consumed by evil.

"It is fate that brought me and my perfect creation together again. She had the perfect body to create the most superior Stalker!" Darmor laughed, showing his teeth. "William and the late Hudson were just prototypes!"

Do all classic villains always tell the heroes their nefarious plans? I thought. *No surprise from Darmor, because he is nuts.*

I once again channeled my mental strength to try to control Darmor. I wanted him to pick up his sword and cut off his own head. I knew that it would be cruel and brutal. But I could not care. I wanted him dead for what he did to Gwendoline.

"And you, the mind-bending one," He was referring to me and he sensed what I was doing. "All my new Stalkers have willpower beyond your control. So don't bother!"

Without any warning, Ross finally shot a bolt at Darmor's unprotected head. Unfortunately, Gwendoline reached out her claws to hit the bolt off course and it thudded on the stairs.

"Now, let's even the odds. Shall we?" Darmor said and he charged towards us with his sword high up in the air. Gwendoline went airborne and followed closely behind him. Ross fired rapidly at Darmor but the shots were ricocheted off Darmor's armor.

When he was within melee range of Ross, Darmor brought the sword down onto his adversary. The blow was devastating as it ripped through Ross's crossbow. Then, Darmor kicked Ross and Ross flew five meters back. Darmor's armor somehow served as a strength boosting exoskeleton.

Darmor brought his blade down again onto Ross but his strike was intercepted by Paige, who'd used her bare hands to clasp the sharp edge of the blade.

"Hello my dear wife. It has been a while." Darmor greeted flirtatiously.

Ross got back on his feet immediately and threw a couple of quick punches at Darmor's face.

As I charged forward to join the skirmish, Gwendoline dived down at me. I took up a vase from the top of a nearby shelf and hurled it at her. Her right wing tilted to the side, and she performed an evasive maneuver and avoided the incoming flying object. I spun and ran, hoping to evade her lethal talons.

But there was no where I could run to. All the doors except the main door, were sealed by titanium grilles. Darmor clearly did not want anyone to trespass into his house. Should I run outside? No, it would be a bad idea as it would make me more vulnerable against an airborne creature.

Gwendoline cornered me. Her claws were ready to tear me apart. I tried manipulating her will but to no avail. She was hungry for me, hungry for my flesh. I repeatedly tried my powers on her. It did not work at all. Her willpower was too strong. Then, I remembered what Darmor just told us moments ago.

All my new Stalkers have willpower beyond your control. So don't bother! He said.

If that was the case, then how did I manage to cease the three leonine beasts from attacking Paige at the front yard? Was it because they were once her beloved dogs?

Gwendoline's wings stopped flapping. She landed onto the ground and marched at me. Her fangs were elongating and she hissed like a serpent. I took up an ornate sculpture from the floor as my final defensive weapon.

Then I remembered what Paige once said to me.

Your powers can only work when the target isn't putting up a mental resistance against it. In other words, don't overly rely on it. She told me.

"Don't overly rely on it." I whispered to myself.

I realized that it was not my powers that prevented the three leonine beasts from attacking Paige earlier. It was Paige's heart and love towards those beasts when they were still her puppies. Somehow among their brainwashed minds, there were definitely scattered memories which they could remember—pleasant memories that the dogs themselves could rhapsodize about.

I gently placed down the ornate sculpture. I took a few steps forward and opened my arms towards Gwendoline. I did this not because I wanted to re-enact what Paige did in order for myself to survive but rather, I wanted to be in Gwendoline's warm embrace when I die.

Gwendoline did not move. Her yellow eyes just stared at me hungrily. Her hideous and demonic face soon faded away in my vision. All I saw was the beautiful, kind, brave and independent girl who I knew. She was standing in front of me and smiling delightfully. I smiled in return and embraced her as tears swelled up my eyes. Artificial human or demon, I loved her just as much.

"I love you Gwen. I love you so much." I sobbed. Then, I thought about my beloved foster mother Aunt Joan. I could feel the smell of the warm breakfast she prepared for me. And then, I saw my little cousins, all three of them together with me playing at the park.

I can die. But my memories with others shall live forever. I told myself.

Slowly shutting my eyes, I tightened my hug on Gwendoline and waited to fall into eternal darkness.

"The true god out there, I thank you for giving me a chance to live this life." I mouthed a quiet prayer. For once in my entire life, I felt that gods were indeed real. The comfort that came to my heart which allowed me to feel at ease with myself, was the greatest blessing ever given. I no longer felt non-religious or non-spiritual from that point of time.

I counted one, two, three, four . . . I should be dead.

"Kob? Is that you?" The sweet voice was difficult to forget.

I opened my eyes and saw the demonic face of Gwendoline. Her facial features were still recognizable beneath the horrible changes. I embraced her tightly.

"Yes! Yes! Yes! Gwen! It's me!" I cried. The amount of happiness that overwhelmed my heart was indescribable

But then, she pushed me away and screamed.

"Run! Kob! I can't hold it . . ." She struggled with her own body. Her claws grabbed some of the robes she was wearing and shredded it apart, exposing her naked demonic body. Her body was similar to a female's, however it was white in color and there were patches of strange bizarre tattoos on it. The tattoos made her looked as if she had undergone some demonic cult rituals.

Then, she released an unearthly shriek and soared up into the high ceiling, smashed though it and vanished into the sky above. I dodged some of the falling debris and sighed.

"No! My perfect Stalker!" Darmor wailed. I should have told him off that his Stalker was not that perfect after all—it failed to kill me.

He had triumphed over Ross and Paige in combat—his opponents were badly beaten up. Now, I was his opponent.

"You will die! Crusano will claim the lives of the unworthy!" Darmor threatened and he lifted up his bloodied sword.

He was undamaged. The armor he was wearing must have protected him well from Ross's and Paige's attacks.

How can I stop him then? I asked myself. Even I could call for help or backup, it would be too late for that.

I noticed Paige. She was barely conscious while her injuries were self-recovering. And I noticed Ross. He was looking at me. He was uncontrollably bleeding. No, that was unimportant. What was important was that he pointed to something and gestured. Then, I began to get his meaning; Darmor was unaware that the back of his armor had been planted explosives. Ross won kudos for his smart tactic.

Now, it must be detonated.

Darmor sprinted at me like a madman he was, brandishing his sword. The armor also gave him enhanced speed. With instinctual reflexes, I rolled to the side and barely evaded the sharp blade. He altered his direction for a second attack.

I deduced that his armor had given him impenetrable defense, gargantuan strength and dazzling speed, unfortunately, it impaired his agility.

Before his second strike hit me, I clicked the detonation button on the explosive devices planted to the back of his armor. There was a loud beep. It signaled the explosives had been activated.

He was taken aback and tried to reach out his arms to remove the explosives. Too bad for him, the armor's structure hindered his articulation. His fingers were not even a centimeter close to those bombs.

"Run! We only have thirty seconds before this whole place blows!" Ross called out to me and he helped Paige onto her feet.

Run!

I was too slow. Darmor's armored hands caught me in the torso. I coughed painfully when he pulled me backwards to deliver a crushing bear hug. I screamed in torment. I could hear the sound of my rib popping.

"You're not getting away. Crusano is here to claim both of us!" He laughed insanely.

My strength was no match against that of his armor. He lifted me off the ground and I started kicking my legs aggressively in mid-air. I was doomed.

Suddenly, he released his grip on me. Paige had delivered a head butt onto his nose. Then, she pounded onto him and clutched him tightly.

"Go Koby! For the sake of those you love." Paige shouted bravely. And she looked passionately at Darmor in the eyes and said to him. "And I will do it for the sake of the one I love. To bring him back on the right path."

Ross dragged me away from them and tugged me behind a large pillar. He braced me against me the pillar. A large ear-splitting explosion came. Fiery gust conquered the entire main hall. The unbearable heat permeated through my skin.

"Paige!" I shouted in despair.

The Aftermath

THE ONCE BEAUTIFUL interior of the mansion changed into a pile of wreckage. Glass fragments, broken wooden, dust and all forms of debris littered the area.

"Are you alright?" Ross asked. He stood up from me, allowing some air for me to breathe.

I nodded without saying a word. There were fragments of glass pieces embedded onto the back of his flak jacket. And there were also fragments pierced into his bloodied hind shoulders. I would have been the one hurt by the fragments if he did not brace against me.

I thanked him.

He nodded without saying a word.

I scavenged through the dense wreckage to look for Paige. Although she had self-healing powers, I knew that she will not survive such an explosion, since such explosions destroy everything within seconds—there was no room for her to regenerate and recover.

She's gone. I understood. *Perhaps right now, she may be having a better husband and happy family somewhere in the afterlife.*

Memories of her came to my mind; memories of how she pretended to be a demon to frighten me away from church, how she became our friend who was always willing to take any damage for us and how she ultimately sacrificed herself to save my life.

I offered her a moment of silence. Ross followed.

When we were done, I brushed the dust off my shirt.

"We'll keep this incident low okay? Auzora organization will follow up from here." Ross said.

"Okay." I replied.

Something within a heap of debris moved.

Paige?

I desperately ran to the heap and started to dig with my bare hands. It was supposedly hurting when glass fragments bit my hands but I did not care, I continued to dig even faster.

It was sadly not Paige. The motion came from Darmor. His armor was destroyed by the explosion along with all his limbs and his face hideously flayed. The remnants of him were his head and upper torso, yet he was still breathing. No doubt the armor he wore mitigated the explosive damage on him, but Paige was not that lucky.

"Paige. Paige. Paige my dear" He mumbled hoarsely. In this state, he was as good as dead.

Ross crouched down onto Darmor's broken body and punched him in the face.

"How many other Stalkers are out there?" He threateningly interrogated the fallen foe.

"I don't know my dear. Maybe Crusano does." Darmor grinned. "Now would you make a meal for me love?"

Ross lost his patience and walloped Darmor violently. I stopped him.

"He has completely lost it. You won't be expecting to get any information out of him." I said. I felt a little too compassionate saying that for all the harm Darmor did to Gwendoline and Paige. But my conscience told me that Darmor had suffered enough already. He won't live much longer, so let him be in peace.

Ross listened to my advice and unclenched his fists. He slowed his breathing to cool down.

"Darmor must quite a lot of those Stalkers other than those in Eropagnis city. We have recent reports on their sightings in other regions." Ross told me and browsed through the LCD screen of his mobile phone.

"Stalkers; you mean like those creatures?" I asked a question which its answer I already knew. The hornet-controlling man William, all the leonine beasts and Gwendoline were Stalkers.

"Yes. Darmor's creation of genetically altered human beings," Ross explained. "His original plan was to make them terrify people so that . . ."

"People will come to him for help. He will be their savior. And he will brainwash them to believe in Crusano." I completed his sentence.

"Exactly. He will only use this backup plan if his fatherly pastor approach fails," Ross continued. "But now, those Stalkers on the loose are the biggest problem. They're like wild animals."

"I am classified as a Stalker too?" I became worried.

"No, you're not as you have not lost your mind," Ross assured me. "To put it simply in my definition, Stalkers are super powered humans with no sense of conscience."

"You will be corrupt one day boy!" Darmor called out unexpectedly. "It will be the day when you realize doing good with that power is meaningless. You will want wealth, fame and . . ."

Darmor's wrinkled eyes closed. He was finally dead.

We left the mansion. Thankfully, no one was near this deserted area as we planned to keep the incident a secret. The birds were chirping melodiously above us on a nearby tree and when I spotted them, they flew off into the blue sky above. I admired the beauty of the sky.

Gwendoline is still out there somewhere. I assured myself and prayed. *May the true god watch over her and make sure she is safe.*

I looked at my watch and switched BRAIN online.

"BRAIN. Do demons really exist?" I casually asked the brilliant artificial intelligence.

"Your question involves the arcane. There are many interpretations about the existence of demons but from my *logical* interpretation . . ." BRAIN replied. ". . . demons can only exist if the human heart unleashes them."

BRAIN was right. Demons are not just made out off evil spirits or genetically mutated species. They are created from the dominant being in our world: humans. The evil "demon" can be within any one of our hearts; even good men can become bad.

It is just waiting for us to unleash it if we are not aware of our own conscience.

Coming on Board

A DARK SHADOWY figure sped out of the darkness without a sound until it was almost behind its preys. When the couple sensed its sinister presence, they nervously spun their heads around to catch a glimpse of their stalker, but to no avail. They firmly held their hands together and started increasing their pace. Words of prayer mumbled from their mouths with the hope that Crusano will save them from this imminent danger. The night was no longer a place for the defenseless. But it was neither street muggers nor thugs that they feared.

It was Jack they feared!

The demon busting and ghost trapping fanatic ambushed them with whole stacks of brochures to promote his demon busting and ghost trapping services.

"Get lost you psycho! You are the demon and ghost yourself!" The girl shouted at him. She turned to her boyfriend and prompted him to say something.

"Yea . . . Go away! We don't need your services, although it sounds kinda cool . . . ," her boyfriend told Jack.

"Indeed as cool as it sounds!" Jack exclaimed.

I poked Jack in his stomach. My little cousins Winston, Kylee and Nicholas followed suit and Jack burst into laughter.

"Come on man! Still advertising for that?" I said.

The couple gave us a weird smile and walked away.

The midterm holiday was here. It was an ideal day to bring my little cousins out for a meal. Back at home, these little rascals were demanding all sorts of junk food but in the end, I'd decided that Chopper's Café would be the finest to dine. Besides, I would be having an appointment with an architect at that café. And so as to help me manage this bunch of young kids, I kindly invited Jack to come along.

Ever since the passing of my dear friend Paige, Jack and I combined some of our savings to pay the landlord in order for us to take over Paige's business. We could not really cook decently enough to live up to the café's reputation, thus we hired Aunt Joan to be our chef. She gladly took up the offer and quitted her job as a clerk to manage the café whenever we were at school. But we did know that Chopper's café will always and forever belong to the great Paige Chopper.

I pushed opened the café door and courteously allowed Jack and my cousins in first. Aunt Joan bade us a welcome. The three little kids rushed to the best sits which were the sofas and hopped onto it. Jack joined them and hollered like a child. It was quite a nuisance in the cozy café but at least it kept the kids entertained.

A bespectacled man in a business outfit sitting at a table waved at me. He was the architect I was expecting. I waved back and took a sit in front of him. He drew a piece of drawing and showed it to me. It was a statue of Paige which looked magnificent. In fact, it will look even more magnificent when its construction is completed at the side of the entrance.

Yes, the architect offered me a very high price for this exquisite statue. The statue was definitely worth the price. Yet unfortunately, I'd to manage the café's budget well. And after countless rounds of bargaining, he finally offered me a reasonable price. I was grateful. But honestly saying, I'd used my powers to decrease his desire for the higher price. Yes, it was like cheating but I was doing it for the café's well-being.

Once the deal was completed, we stood up and shook hands. Then, he left.

Jack came up to sit me beside me.

"Well, I guess we'll still see Paige after the construction of the statue is completed huh?" Jack said and he rested a bandaged hand on the table.

"I believe we will always see her within our hearts." I smiled.

There was a commotion outside the café at the alleyway. There was a group of people marching towards the streets. They're an angry mob holding signs and posters. Jack and I walked out to take a closer look.

The mob consisted of protesters. They were protesters against Crusanity. There were harsh remarks about Crusanity and Crusano himself.

"Crusano is the devil!"

"Crusanity is a dangerous cult!"

"The Followers are hypocritical lackeys!"

I felt hurt by these remarks even though I was not a zealous religionist, because it was really unfair of them to stereotype Crusanity due of the failure of some Followers. Indeed although the pastor was a disgrace, his actions were done out of his own malice, madness and cruel ambitions. It had little or almost nothing to do with the religion itself.

All religions are intrinsically good. It is people who shape it based on their own character. I thought.

Once the commotion was over, we turned back to enter the café but three individuals intercepted our path.

One of them was Ross. The others were unfamiliar to us; a tall burly man with a goatee and a handsome woman with blonde hair. All three of them wore a dark brown coat.

"Koby. This is Derek Smite and Leah Cross." Ross introduced the other two to me. They reached out their hands for mine. I shook them firmly. But when Jack reached out his, they withdrew theirs. Jack shrugged in embarrassment.

"Ross, what's this about?" I asked.

"I'm offering you a job to be a member of Auzora. Your superhuman abilities will be an asset to our organization. And you'll be paid well." He replied. Then I was right—those two were indeed from his organization. I could already tell from their expression; a look of seriousness and mental focus, to be constantly on the lookout for threats. And they will be the ones to hunt the threats down, one by one.

Ross reached into his coat and handed me a short sword.

The blade was bluish silver metal with a unique leaf-shaped design. It looked sharp and lethal. It reeked of death.

"A little gift from us if you are coming on board," Ross offered. "What say you?"

"Wow! Jack wants in! Jack wants in!" Jack volunteered. I'd told him what I've learnt about the Auzora organization.

"We need people who are willing to risk their lives for the sake of many others. We don't want hyperactive adolescents." Ross protested.

Jack wanted to help. I was confident he could.

"He has genius-level intellect. He will be a great asset too. I can vouch for him." I justified Jack's worth. Yet the worth of his genuine friendship far outweighed the worth of his intelligence.

"Okay then. You can help out. But don't blame me if you die." Ross reluctantly agreed.

Jack jumped up straight into the air and cheered aloud.

"Now we're done with him. What about you Koby?" Ross asked me again.

Then, Gwendoline came to my mind. She had become a winged demon and her whereabouts were unknown. But I could not give up on her. The Auzora organization will give me the opportunity and means to track her down. Even if they must kill her, I wanted to be there for her as I've faithfully promised her. I looked back at Ross, wrapped my fingers around the new weapon and took it from his hand. It was light but deadly. Then I said,

"I'm in."